UMFAAN'S HEROES

UMFAAN'S HEROES

JON ELKON

ANDRE DEUTSCH

First published in Great Britain 1989 by
André Deutsch Limited
105–106 Great Russell Street London WC1B 3LJ

British Library Cataloguing in Publication Data

Elkon, Jon
Umfaan's heroes.
I. Title
823[F]

ISBN 0 233 98361 9

Printed and bound in Great Britain
by WBC Bristol and Maesteg

To Really Good Bennett: *Né?*

One

Hallo. My name is Thomas Bloch. I am lying in a bed in a military hospital. This is 1967. This body I am wearing is full of holes, dents, cuts and bruises. It is slowly growing together again. And when it is satisfactorily regrown, they are going to hang it.

Around me bustles the army camp called Tempe, in the middle of that blood and sweat and tear-stained country called South Africa: a stupid name for a country. It will be called Azania after the Revolution.

This body is smallish, about five foot ten – but it's a well-formed thing with good proportions and I would be happy with it if it weren't for the pain. The hair is a little too fuzzy and the nose just a bit too big. I will have just turned seventeen when they hang me.

I entered this body at ten in the morning in February 1949. This was a good time to be born, as this early in the morning there was a fresh shift of doctors and nurses in the Brentwood Nursing Home, so they didn't fuck up my grand entrance. So I'm an Aquarian, one of

1

the people for whom this current age is supposed to have been made. I haven't as yet come across any evidence to support this theory.

I want to tell you how I got here, how I ended up in this hospital, and why all these people keep pestering me with their stupid questions.

It began when I met Pieter. Or when we met Absolom. Or when my mother met my father. Or when the world began.

I sometimes think that I know everything, see everything, remember all my past lives, can see into other people's past lives, am, in other words, omniscient and possibly God. Pieter tells me that I cannot possibly be God, as he was told on good authority that God was killed by a number 37 bus in 1973. Since this is in the future, I will have to explain all that. Or I will let Pieter do it.

I don't really have the time to trace the history of the earth and show how it landed me here sore all over. Also, I can't get enough paper in this stupid place. I have to beg Nurse Van Tonder to get it for me. She isn't sympathetic. 'Why you got to waste your time on this? Why you don't write to your mother?'

Mommy and Daddy came to visit me last week, when I still had bandages wrapped around most of me. All I wanted was a piss, and I couldn't call Van Tonder to bring the bottle because that would offend the parents. As a result I must have seemed pretty rude. Mother left in tears. I always manage to squeeze water out of her for some reason. It's never my fault.

Time warp. Johannesburg 1948. Everything in black and white except for a couple of specks of pallid colour. A grimy smoke-smeared station. Full of all races of swarming people and loud with the Ouf-*wheeze*! of steamtrains pulling in and out.

A particular train. They called it the Blue Train. Its

carriages are squeaky-clean and panelled in yellow-wood and mahogany and the First Class carriages are modelled on the Orient Express.

We have to pass those and go to the Second Class. I'll spare you the Third Class because that's too much like India. A particularly handsome young man at a train window, bidding his mother goodbye. She is pressing packages into his reluctant hands – cold chicken, biscuits, sandwiches, tomatoes already splitting and musty boiled eggs flaking bits of calcium dandruff. Little Jewish lady in a shawl, her eyes with tears. Inside the carriage, his best friend Phil who has no mother is bidding a noisy and embarrassing goodbye to a girl-friend.

Handsome Danny is embarrassed because he's twenty-eight years old and unmarried, and his mother is making a scene. He is in the process of becoming a successful businessman in a very small way – with rocking horses. He gives his mama more than half his earnings. She thinks he's a bit funny – but vunderful. She also thinks he's crazy to work so hard when he should be going out and finding a pretty Jewish girl to marry.

She wipes a tear with a corner of her shawl. At least, I suppose she did, in official Jewish mama fashion. 'Are you sure you're all right, Danny. Are you sure you've got everything.'

'Yes yes, as long as everything's all right with you.'

'Don't you worry about your mama. I looked after me and your father and you with nothing. Why shouldn't I be all right?'

'Well, look after yourself . . .'

'Don't you worry. I looked after before you gave me the ten pounds a weak. I can look after for three weeks.'

Daniel is annoyed again. She could always turn any discussion into a guilt-laden bog.

'Have you brought the shirt I bought you?' She means the new yellow silk shirt she bought out of her

3

housekeeping – which Daniel gives her. She had ironed it with a cool iron, and folded it and left it on Danny's bed so that he would find it when he got home from work. Danny had seen it there, been annoyed, and had a gravy-match with her over dinner.

'Yes.'

'Have you brought your yarmulka? There must be a shul there.'

'Oh God, Mama, I'm not going to shul on holiday—'

'Wash your mouth!' The train jerks and whistles. Or perhaps the guard whistles. 'Have a vunderful time! And go to shul, hear?'

Fluttering handkerchiefs. Steam. Shrieking from Marcia inside the carriage as she realises that the train is going too fast for her to alight . . . and Danny's friend Phil has removed most of her clothes. Marcia was the only person who had come to say goodbye to Phil. Both his parents had died in a car crash when he was five. Now he sold insurance, moderately successfully, and had developed a wide-boy image to go with the profession. Twirly moustache, wide-lapelled suit, natty hat. He was also Danny's best friend and had involved my father-to-be in many scrapes in their army days.

Mama hated him. Partly because he wasn't Jewish.

What Phil and Danny did with Marcia between Johannesburg and Kroonstad, the next station – where she staggered off in giggly déshabillé – will not be told here.

Danny was amazingly good-looking at that time. I found a photograph of him from his army days in Gran's shed. Brown, Jewish-curly hair framing a Rupert Brooke face with that terribly attractive air-brushed blush in the cheeks.

Let's go back to Johannesburg station two days later.

A chauffeur-driven Bentley draws up at the entrance. Black chauffeur with a deep-faced, moth-eaten look.

The car is nearly as moth-eaten as its driver. It's nine years old. Cancerous rust-spots bloom between paint and metal. The leather seats are seamed and lined like an old Eskimo.

On the back seat is a pale, thin girl of nineteen. Her make-up is sparse and smudged with recent tears. Her hair hangs naturally over bony shoulders. She looks like a white rose in an antique velvet-lined box.

She leans forward, placing her elegant little hand confidentially on the back of Jim's seat. 'Thank you, Jim.' She tips forward a tiny bit more and drops a half-crown on to his lap. He pockets it so quickly it appears to vanish into another dimension.

'I'll carry the bag,' he says, making no move to get out or open her door or carry her bag.

'No, don't worry. I'll get a porter,' she says, knowing Jim wants to get back as quickly as possible.

Jim wants to get back before the Wicked Stepmother discovers that he has used the family Bentley to convey her acquired relative to the station.

(Jim lost his job when he returned. The Wicked Stepmother was furious that Jim hadn't been there when she had wanted to go shopping. She justified the sacking to her husband by listing Jim's real and imaginary faults and misdemeanours. He nodded and sighed and said Yes Dear and lost an old friend.

'Please be careful, Miss Anne,' says Jim. He loves the young miss, though he thinks her too thin. He loves the way her little tits bob about in the yellow (yes yellow) silk blouse. He has loved her for ten years. When she had left home a year ago after an argument with Hazel (she had wanted to go to university and the W.S. had resisted because of what she had considered to be Horrific Costs) Jim had clandestinely helped her move to the flat she shared with a friend I'll call Sylvia, because I've forgotten her name. Only Jim and Anne's father knew that Anne was working for a rather radical bookshop in town. Had the W.S. known that she would have died with shame.

'It's only a holiday, Jim,' she laughed. 'Sylvia will meet me at Muizenberg station. I'll be all right.' She alights elegantly. She goes to the boot and lugs out the huge trunk. She staggers around to the driver's window. 'Goodbye, Jim.' He doesn't answer. He puts the car in gear and drives off with a fugitive tear losing itself in the ploughed ridges of his honest face. Goodbye, Jim.

Anne goes off to meet her fate in Muizenberg.

And to meet my father-to-be.

She was independent and brave for her time. Going on a 1,000-mile journey alone wasn't usual for young ladies from Johannesburg's Northern Suburbs. Not that she would meet too much danger in First Class.

In 1948 General Smuts and the United Party lost the general election. In the post-war era it was common for the people to throw off the heroic governments who had led them in war.

In South Africa the Blacks, Coloureds, Indians, Bushmen and Jews quaked. The latter quaked because the incoming Nationalists had openly supported the Nazis during the war. Many had been interned – including John Vorster, who became Prime Minister much later.

For the browner races, things looked black indeed.

By that date the Blacks were becoming more militant and the official implementation of the Apartheid policy consolidated resistance. While the majority of them were scattered over the country in little subsistence-economy communities, there were also growing townships all around the industrial centres. Since the 'thirties, young Blacks had been flowing into the townships in search of money, food, booze and sex away from the rigid tribal laws. Their ramshackle dwellings riddled with children, dogs, scrawny chickens. By the 'sixties, the crime rate in Soweto outstripped New York.

The Afrikaners weren't the first authors of black misery. They were carrying on a long colonial tradition. It was the English-dominated administration who, in 1936, removed black voting rights. In exchange they allocated 13 per cent of the country to the Blacks.

Even in 1948 some of the Whites realised, with a prickle at the back of their necks, that one day the Blacks would have a revenge that would never be forgotten. Anne and Daniel knew. They both hated the Nationalists and their racism. It was something they had in common, on that beach at Muizenberg and ever afterwards.

I don't know what the first words they said to each other were. I do know that at one stage there was something like a life-or-death battle between Danny and Phil for Anne's attention. Poor Phil ended up with too-fat Sylvia, three kids, a divorce, a massive bankruptcy and then, inevitably, suicide.

Muizenberg was a valiant attempt by Victorians to re-create Brighton in Africa. They built a wondrous sea-encroaching pier covered in wrought-iron scrolls and foliation. They built white stuccoed beachfront hotels, where Coloured waiters clucked and fussed over the rich fat moneybags from Joeys and their kids. Unfortunately the illusion was wrecked by the forty-foot waves and the beach of real sand.

On the day Anne and Daniel met, the white beach was a flurry of multi-coloured umbrellas, children, nannies and white folks generally stuffing themselves with cakes and sandwiches.

Further up the coast was a beach for Blacks. No chalets. Just a few umbrellas.

Anne and Daniel didn't think about *them* at all.

Two

A living room in the white suburb of Parktown, Johannesburg. The houses in Parktown are huge sprawling Victorian-Gothic monsterpieces with turrets, towers, stained glass, built by the early nouveau-riche gold and business barons. (I saw them again recently. Some are the headquarters of major companies. Others have been turned into burger restaurants. A few have become studios for spoiled students to use while they are playing hippy and the rest are either biodegrading or have vanished and been replaced by private clinics for the very rich.)

The Wicked Stepmother and the Henpecked Husband. I'll call them Hazel and Robert. She was on the sofa, he sat at the desk trying to ignore the nasty facts emerging from the accounts of the business. She wore lace and pearls. He wore a waistcoat and checked trousers. Mary brought the coffee. They had just eaten a magnificent meal Mary had spent all afternoon preparing. He had not eaten his peas.

Mary put the tray on the stinkwood table. Her eyes were lowered. They saw only the table's polished surface, its ball-and-claw feet, the pale Aubusson carpet. She was thinking only of Absolom, her son, in prison.

Robert was a gentle, balding, paunchy man in his forties. He sighed because he was finally having to admit to himself that he would have to sell another hotel. Which would leave him only two – the Grant in Vereeniging and Stones' in Johannesburg. The last thing he wanted to do was tell her. But she would have to know.

He would never sell Stones'. Stones' had been the first proper hotel in Johannesburg. It was built in 1890, four years after the founding of the town that grew on the fat, rich reef of gold God had, for some reason, given to that part of Africa. Stones' was panelled, stained-glass, mahogany and marble. He could still remember miners coming into the bar in filthy clothes, slamming bags of gold dust on the counter and ordering his father to provide drinks all round. He remembered excellent fights, too. Hollywood missed a golden (oops) opportunity when it decided to glorify the American cowboy instead of these rugged ragged fortune-seekers, the gold-maddened prospectors of South Africa.

'I think I'll have to start to crochet, or maybe knit,' Hazel said as if she were continuing a long-running argument. She's feeling ignored.

Robert sighs. 'It's no good, dear, we'll have to do it,' he said, continuing a long-running argument of his own. 'What?' he asked, suddenly aware that she had said something first.

'I can't stand it anymore, Robert.'

'What?'

'Do you know the swimming pool has had a crack in it since we were married?'

'What has that to do with your taking up crochet, dear?'

'You don't have to pretend to be stupid with me, Robert. Do you realise we haven't been out in a month?'

'Yes dear. You were feeling ill.'

'I was. I am. And how can I invite people here if we haven't got any water in the pool?'

'Perhaps you should see the doctor again, dear.' This could go on for hours, he thought.

'I *have* seen the doctor again,' she said tartly. There was a slight, bitter silence as she waited for him to ask her what the doctor had said, and he waited for her to tell him.

He decided to take advantage of the pause to change the well-worn ruts of this discussion. 'There's something I have to tell you—'

9

'You *still* aren't listening!'

'If you would let me finish—'

'I'm going to have a baby.'

The announcement cut through his mind like a sliver of ice. It froze his stillborn confession. He tried to recall when they had last slept together. Was she young enough to have a baby? 'How – how long—'

'Is that all you have to say?'

'Darling, I—'

'I told you I had to have a baby, didn't I? Well, now I'm going to have one. It's confirmed. A brother or sister for Anne.'

Robert is absorbed in his own thoughts, trying to adapt to this incredible news, integrate it into his knowledge that the money was running out, trying to work out how his routine would be affected . . .

Hazel was crying. 'You don't *care*, do you?' He melted. Left the desk and embraced her. They cried together. Robert for the loss of what was left of his freedom. Hazel because she wanted attention.

When Anne and Danny returned from their respective holidays they continued to see each other. Secretly, of course! The daughter of the Stones couldn't be seen in public with a poor Jewboy. So they met in friends' flats, in cars, in parks and decided that they were in love. Having decided *that*, it took a mere three weeks to decide to get married.

The idea appealed terrifically to Anne because it was such a daring, rebellious, romantic thing to do. It appealed to Daniel because he had always wanted to marry a rich shiksa.

The truth is, they *were* in love a bit; and the longer they lived together, the more in love they became. Albeit very slowly.

Imagine the scenes when these two have to tell their parents. They talked about it a great deal, and came to no conclusions. The simple fact was, each would have to have a pretty stiff drink and.

Anne rang Robert at the hotel. 'Hallo, dear,' said Robert. 'So you're back?'

'A month ago, Daddy. I rang you, remember?'

'I'm sorry, darling, I've been so busy. We have a bit of a crisis here as usual. And the bloody baby—'

'What baby?'

'Hazel's having one, silly woman. Didn't I tell you?'

'Oh Daddy!' Anne is delighted, and also rather amused. 'That's lovely!'

'Is it? Oh good. I'm not that keen, though, they make a hellish noise and the *smell*—'

'Stop trying to pretend you're not thrilled. Anyway congrats!'

'Thank you, I think.'

'I've got news that will add to your cup.'

'What cup?'

'Your cup of *joy*, darling.'

He laughed. 'You're going to get married,' he said.

'Daddy, you're wonderful!'

'I know. Why? Oh hell, I mean, you're not, are you?'

'Yes I am! Gosh, you're clever!'

'What's his name?'

Suddenly the conversation slowed down like a train getting to the incline. 'Daniel, Daddy. Daniel Bloch.'

'Bloch? Isn't that a Jewish name?'

'Yes. Daniel is Jewish, Papa.'

Silence for thought. Then, 'Well, thank God!'

'Why thank God?'

'Thank God he isn't Black!' Father and daughter laugh together though daughter is not really amused. Just relieved.

She told him how they had met, some of their adventures, what Danny did for a living, who his parents were – all the important stuff. Except who would tell Hazel. They both knew that she would scream and throw fits and anything else lying around.

That words like 'shame' and 'typical' would scythe around the room. And, 'What will people think?'

Robert did one of the three courageous things he had ever done. 'I had better tell your stepmother,' he said. 'It *could* be better coming from me.'

'Yes, Daddy,' said Anne, with intense relief.

Hazel didn't throw a thing. She had given up on Anne years ago. She had tried to win the girl, had failed. She was far more interested in the little sod trying to escape from her belly.

They did have a row later though, about whether Hazel should have a new dress for the occasion. Robert felt that she should. Hazel said it would be quite ridiculous. Who would dress up for such a wedding? Nobody would come, anyway, and what was the sense of buying a dress which would be redundant when she was no longer pregnant? And so on.

Danny didn't have such an easy time.

Meet Danny's father. His name is Mosheh in Hebrew. People call him Mossie. He is grey and shrunken and wears his hair scraggy and long to match his beard. He wears trousers which come up to his chest and are suspended by braces. His shirt is white and missing a collar. His hand shakes as he puts the soup spoon down. Other soup spoons hang suspended, their wielders – Mama, Danny, Lionel – wait for the grenade to go off.

Mama is preparing to weep.

'Tell me what you're saying in pure English. Are you saying she's not Jewish?'

'I'm saying she's not Jewish.'

'What's wrong with you?' Mossie half stands. The soup spoons tink on to the plates.

'What do you mean—'

12

'Don't ask me what do I mean, you know what I mean!' The grenade finally goes off. 'How can you do this to me? To your mother! We brought you up on nuppence! You and that lazy brother of yours! Didn't I bring you up Jewish? How can you—'

'*Please*, Mossie,' says Mama through tears.

'*Look* what you've done to your mother!' He stands, the chair flies backward, crash! 'I could bash your stupid *face* – LEAVE this house!'

Daniel stands too. 'I don't want to say this, but you're making me. Remember, Father, who's *paying* for this house!'

Mossie slams out of the room and bangs the door leaving tears and soup going cold.

Bigotry wasn't Mossie's predominant characteristic. He was just a religious man who took the Torah literally and though no saint, he was an ascetic who spent much of his time in study and meditation. He was also an intellectual, but his mind was stuck in Lithuania 1901.

And Mama wasn't just a weepy woman. She was a very strong character really, but her favourite weapon was Tears. She used them more powerfully than Alexander the Great used his sword. In this way she was very like Anne.

Come to think of it, Hazel wasn't really a Wicked Stepmother. She was certainly ambitious. But she did love Robert. She loved to mother him. She had lived for forty years with an unfulfilled yearning for a child. So of course she resented Anne.

It goes without saying that Robert wasn't just a Henpecked Husband. He was a number of other things as well. Like compassionate, intelligent and convinced of the inherent *goodness* of everyone.

Mary Molapo was of the Northern Sotho tribe. Her

father Nelson had brought her, her mother and five other children with him when he went to Johannesburg in 1939. South Africa's war effort (did you know that South Africa decided to enter the war by only twelve votes in Parliament?) had created a need for a cheap, compliant labour force. The result was a flood of hopeful Blacks to the townships.

Mary sat in her little room at the bottom of the Stones' garden. There is a lithograph of Mary the Virgin Mother on the wall in a chipped plaster frame. Her bed is covered with a Basuto blanket. The bedstead is iron. A two-bar electric heater sizzles moths, though it is not cold.

Mary leant back in the rickety armchair with the broken arm and re-read the letter from her son Absolom. It was five years old. Au! What a clever boy to write English and to speak Sotho and Afrikaans.

> My Mother I have been in the school all day
> and I am not very happy. Grandfather is very
> old these days, but he is very well. The mealie
> crop is good this year and who will gather it?
> The girls are both well and send their love.
>
> My mother when will you come again? We
> want to see you. Will you please bring the
> takkies, I have no shoes any more.

Mary laughed. Her Absolom had grown since then. She hugged the letter. Her mind sought Absolom's father, John. He was in the mines somewhere, she didn't know where. She hadn't known for five years.

The door opened. '*Dumela owsie*!' A young man with a check cap entered, grinning broadly beneath a struggling moustache. 'Are we open for business?'

'Are you drunk already, James?' She asked, putting the letter gently on the table, like an injured dove.

'My sister, I have only just finished work!'

'Sit down.' He sat lankily on the bed and leaned back.

14

She reached under it and withdrew a large tin container, the lower half of what had once been an oil drum. Now it frothed with a creamy white substance smelling of rotted mealies, paraffin and death. She dipped an enamel mug into the beer, filled it and passed it to him.

He gulped down two generous mouthfuls, wiped his mouth with the back of his sleeve and sighed deeply with vast, unaffected relief. He stretched out further. 'Ai!' he said, eyeing her with mock lasciviousness. 'You are looking good, you know?'

'Have your beer and be quiet,' she said, laughing.

He took a more considered gulp. Suddenly he was serious. 'What's happened to your Absolom now? Has he been to the court?'

Her eyes lowered and grief rose up in her. 'I don't think so, they say they are taking him to court on Thursday.'

'He was stupid to steal.'

'Yes, and stupid to get caught.' She buried her head in her hands and sobbed.

The door opened and Joseph came in. He was the sixty-year-old gardener. He was grey and lined and dressed in ill-fitting cast-offs from Robert's wardrobe.

'Hallo,' he said, 'what's this crying? Have you heard something?' She nodded dumbly.

'Thursday,' said James.

'It is a sad thing,' said Joseph sagely and sat on the bed next to James. 'Never mind, sister.' He leaned forward and placed a dry hand on her shoulder. 'I have a present!' and he withdrew a half bottle of Robert's whisky from his pocket.

Mary was built like a giraffe. She had long, thin legs and a long thin neck. In 1948 she was thirty-eight years old. She had a well-rounded rear, which made her popular with the men who visited her little shebeen in the little room at the bottom of the garden. In those days alcohol was forbidden to the Blacks. As with Prohibition in the US, this simply resulted in people using the ingenuity they could have been expending on improving their lot on maintaining a dignified level of insobriety.

Mary, despite her contempt for the liquor laws, was a religious woman. Every Thursday, her one day off in the week, she would travel to the township where she would change into the starched uniform of the *Manyano*, the women's Prayer League. She would pray for peace, for her family, for love. She would raise money for the legion of poor who inhabited Alexandria, Soweto and Dube.

Chatting with the women in the hall, she would join in the shaking heads and wagging tongues as they condemned the crime which flourished there like pimples on a teenager.

This week she would not go to the Manyano. She couldn't face chubby Mrs Nukala, or Mrs Mothle with her prim, shrill voice. She didn't want to hear their sympathetic clucks when she told them about Absolom.

'You know what I think,' said wise Joseph, a little later that night, 'I think the Master is going bankrupt!'

'I know how he feels,' said Mary.

Three

Mossie wouldn't speak to Danny at all. This created an unbearable atmosphere at home. Daniel's youngest brother Lionel didn't resent his marrying a Christian as much as he resented his own solo state. But he did resent the atmosphere at the dining table at Shabat, when all the family traditionally ate together. He also resented the strain poor Mama was under. It showed in her every movement as she slopped plates in front of them (their only servant, the villainous Dirk, was never allowed to serve on the Sabbath). She would sit opposite Mossie, glaring alternately at the two combatants, daring them to have a conversation.

Anne's parents accepted the situation. There are a few obvious reasons for this. For one thing Hazel's pregnancy seemed to have watered down her normally abrasive and domineering personality. And, Anne wasn't living at home which meant that, unlike Daniel, she didn't have to feel guilty at the dinner table.

Most important: Robert adored Anne, and for him anything she did was OK.

Anne and Daniel sit on the couch in the Stones' living-room. Hazel sits in the deep armchair. She is engaged in inefficient crochet-work. Robert sits awkwardly in the straight-backed chair which is normally facing the desk. Now it faces the tense little group. Mary brings coffee. She has been crying again. There is silence until, without once looking up, she has placed the tray on the sofa-table and withdrawn.

'Tell me properly now, young man,' says Robert, conscious of his duty as father of the bride-to-be.

'It's all right, Robert,' says Hazel, looking up dangerously. 'You don't have to interrogate the boy.'

Robert is defensive. 'I only wanted—' His protest is swallowed up by the silence.

'I'm – uh – a managing director,' says Daniel.

Hazel leans forward with exaggerated effort and pours the coffee.

'Of what?' she asks suddenly, interrupting the decisions about milk and sugar.

Daniel has forgotten the context. 'Oh, um – of my company.'

'Yes, I know that. Tell us about your company.' Hazel wants confirmation of the information she has received via the family lawyer.

'I – make toys.'

'Really?' Robert asks, to show that he has been listening.

'Yes, dear,' Hazel confirms. 'Rocking horses.'

Anne's voice cuts in. 'Don't you want to know what his father does?' She is faintly sarcastic but this is lost on Hazel.

'I know that, dear. *You* told us all about that.'

'What does your father do?' Robert asks, as if he has just thought of the question.

'Nothing. I mean – he works in a bicycle shop.' Danny is referring to the occasional help Mossie gives to his friend Issy, who owns a bicycle repair shop. Issy loves Mossie's company and their endless game of 'Ain't it awful'.

'You didn't tell us *that*!' Hazel has just triumphed over Anne. 'I knew anyway.'

Anne ignores Hazel's rising score. 'Have some more coffee,' she says, pointedly pouring for Danny alone.

'We would love to meet your parents,' Robert says politely.

Daniel's heart sinks through the soles of his Italian shoes. Anne sends him a look which says both I beg you not to think Daddy is an idiot, and I told you so; Robert replies with a look that says Oh God, he doesn't mean it, does he?

Anne comes to the rescue. 'They're ill, Daddy. Old and ill.'

'Both of them? How sad. Still, when they're better, you must invite them round.' Robert leans back, smugly convinced that he has done the Right Thing. Anne sends him a look which means, I'll get you later.

Hazel extends temporary relief. 'Where are you going to live after your marriage? Have you thought about that yet?'

'We – we haven't decided.' Anne's hand seeks Daniel's.

'Tell me something frankly, young man – man to man. Have you any money?'

Anne is writhing.

'No sir,' says Daniel, feeling warmth from this man and grateful for it. 'All my money's tied up – in the business.' Robert nods; understanding has been established between these men of the world. Robert approves.

Hazel breaks the spell. Looks up from the hopeless tangle of purple wool. 'How do you propose getting married on no money?'

'I'll make money eventually. I know I will.' Maintaining charm and confidence at all costs.

Robert's admiration grows. Though he loves Hazel, he also likes to see her challenged. 'You can stay here for a while,' he says, proud of himself for having solved a weighty problem with one decisive stroke. 'We have plenty of room,' he continues, ignoring his wife's burgeoning dismay. 'We have two spare bedrooms, even after the baby.'

This was the temporary solution Anne had hoped for. She is playing a tactical game. It is a game she has played before with success. 'Daddy, you're very kind,' she says, 'but I do have my flat—'

'*Which* you share,' she says testily, acknowledging defeat. 'What do you think Sylvia will feel about having two of you in that little place?'

'Perhaps I can find her somewhere else—'

'And how will you pay the rent?' Hazel asks. She has decided that their moving in is her idea. Besides, Anne could be useful when the baby comes. 'All *his* money is in his business.'

Robert knows the game. He decides to play it to the hilt. 'Perhaps you're right, Anne,' he says. 'It could be difficult with two women in the kitchen.'

'Oh what rubbish, Robert. Have you ever *seen* me in

19

the kitchen?' Robert laughs. 'Or Anne, for that matter. What do you think we have servants for?'

Pause while the combatants consider their next moves.

'Besides,' Hazel continues, 'it was bad enough you living in Hillbrow with a flatmate – what will our friends think if we let the two of you starve in your little garret?'

Anne shrugs

'It's settled then,' Hazel says smugly, her victory assured. 'You'll live here. At least until you can afford somewhere respectable.'

Anne's hand tightens in Daniel's. He is unsettled by the idea. They will argue furiously about it later. He is worried about *his* parents' shame. He is unhappy that *he* won't be providing their first home. But he will yield to her because she will point out how easily he will be able to adapt to a swimming pool, a one-acre garden and five servants.

This argument happened in the back seat of Robert's limo, which was ferrying the young lovers to their respective homes. That night a violent thunderstorm dumped tons of water onto the Highveld. Johannesburg's thunderstorms are brief but incredibly violent. Wars of the gods. In this storm two Blacks were killed by lightning. Three more were killed when their corrugated-iron shacks got in the way of the raging water. A ten-year-old Afrikaans boy was drowned on a farm in Rivonia. His name was Hennie Marais.

The storm made driving impossible and Boetie, the Stones' new chauffeur, had stopped the car half-way, refusing to drive until he could see where he was going. So my parents-to-be had an hour to have the hoarse-voiced, half-whispered discussion already summarised.

The storm died down and Daniel finally got home at twelve. To meet another storm.

Mossie, a cup of half-drunk cold coffee before him, was maintaining a lone vigil in the lounge, sitting like a dead moth amidst the antimacassars.

Daniel was soaked. He pulled his dripping coat off and hung it on the coat stand. Turning, he saw the glint-eyes of the old man glaring at him across the murky room. His heart flipped. 'Hallo, Dad,' he said, not expecting an answer.

'So you come home at last. Your rich friends have all gone to bed, have they?'

'You're *talking* to me?' Daniel approached cautiously.

'Sit!' Mossie ordered. 'Yes, I'm talking to you. Unless you listen to me, it will be the last time.'

'I've heard it all before, Father. You have to understand that I am in *love*—'

'I am your *father*! Hear what I have got to say!' Spittle sprayed across the room.

Daniel stood, arms crossed. 'Won't you even *meet* her?'

'If you bring that—! Shut your insolent mouth and *sit*!'

Daniel obeyed. There was no choice. Jagged lightning flashed outside, followed by an angry thunderclap. Mossie leaned forward, placing a reluctant shaking crumpled hand on Daniel's. 'My boy, it is even possible she's a very nice girl. I know it is possible. But you must understand the Law—'

'The Law . . .' Daniel sighs.

'The Law which says that a child with a non-Jewish mother is *not* a Jew. Do you understand?'

Daniel shook his head, looked into the old man's eyes, nearly cried.

'I have also studied Torah, Father—'

'Nothing would make me and your mama more happy than you should marry—'

21

'I know. A Nice Jewish Girl—'

'Yes. A nice Jewish girl. This is an infatuation only. You'll live—'

Daniel snatched his hand away. 'I *love* her, Dad. Don't you know what that is?'

Mossie's anger is rising again. 'Love! What is this love? If I worried about *love* when I married Mama I wouldn't be so happy now. My marriage was arranged by a *professional* in the shtetl. He looked for a girl who would suit me perfectly, with the right *parents*, with the right money, everything was taken care of by an older and wiser person with years of experience—'

'I am old enough to know what I want! You *won't* interfere. Those days are gone—' Suddenly they were both standing. The armistice was over.

'Don't tell me old enough! I will tell you something, my boy.' Eyes four inches apart from each other's, breathing in each other's breath. 'If you marry that girl I will not speak another word to you. For the rest of my life. Understand?'

'Why are you so bloody stupid?' Daniel asked.

'Get out of here! Go to your room! If this wasn't your house I would kick you out!'

Daniel went to bed. Like Mossie, he seethed all night. Unlike Mossie, he was alive in the morning.

Yes, Mossie died that night. One of those thunderclaps was for him. Mama just turned over in bed. She had been woken by what she had thought was sobbing. She embraced him. He was cold and dead. She leapt up screaming.

Well, it was all very sad and guilt-laden, and maybe Mossie's ghost was appeased by a brilliant compromise: Anne decided to convert to Judaism. A long road of learning Hebrew, going to classes, studying at home for hours every day.

Mama was inconsolable. Lionel took two weeks off from college in Bloemfontein and moved back home to help Daniel with the difficult task of keeping her alive. Dust gathered in the house. She wouldn't allow Dirk to do his usual token clean-up. The carpet gathered little rolls of fluff. The wallpaper discoloured, peeled. She wanted the house kept just as it was on the night when, as she secretly believed, Daniel killed his father. She wasn't able to be alone with Daniel for any length of time without breaking into tears.

After a decent interval, Daniel and Anne announced a date for the wedding. It would take place in June. In May, Anne realised that she was pregnant. That was me, impatient to get on with the story.

Mama found out. I don't know how. Perhaps Anne confided in her in a desperate attempt to win her. Luckily, the discovery that she was pregnant coincided rather nicely with her official conversion to Judaism. Mama was happy, and sad, and confused. She told Mossie both pieces of news one night. She had regular conversations with Mossie long after his death. He had decided to hang about a bit to see how things turned out. The news pleased him so much that he began looking around for another Jewish body to inhabit.

Hazel and Robert accepted their daughter's new religion, her slightly pregnant state and everything else. They even had a magnificent marquee wedding in their garden, which amazed their friends considering that the ceremony had been a Jewish one. The wedding also put a final full stop on Robert's accounts. The Vereeniging hotel had to go.

The Fort in Johannesburg has never actually been a fort, that is, a military emplacement built for defence. Once (it was May 25th, 1900) the Boers manned the place

23

briefly as the British approached Johannesburg. Then they surrendered. Nowadays the Fort is a vast underground prison complex. A mound of earth is the only feature which identifies its existence above the ground, apart from the heavy wooden gates and a slit window through which would-be visitors can plead with implacable khaki-uniformed guards.

Mary Molapo sat on a creaky wooden chair in a large, badly-lit room which is divided in half by a steel grille. On the other side of the bars her son Absolom sat on an identical chair. He was twenty-two, powerfully built, dressed in regulation prison blues. It would be impossible for a casual observer to mistake the relationship between prisoner and visitor. Her long bones translated into his male body perfectly, and looked right covered with good muscle.

'It wasn't a crime, Mother. You must let me tell you exactly what happened.'

'Why do you make this sorrow for your mother? Absolom, I slaved to give you education. Why you think I sent you to the Catholic School? I wanted you to be—'

'Hold my hand, Mother.' He poked one hand dangerously through the bars. She held it between her own and glanced guiltily at the guard who pretended not to notice. 'Please listen.'

She sniffed. 'All right. Tell me.'

'Mother, you know they will ban us. They don't like Blacks involved in politics.'

'You were arrested for *thieving*, my son.'

'Mother, they know me, these police. I was walking through the street. I was minding my own business. Two men ran up. They threw a parcel at me. They were running from the law. The law ran up to me. They caught me and put on handcuffs. They called me a "thieving kaffir".'

'Are you lying to me?' She looked him in the eyes. She knew he couldn't lie to her.

24

'No, Mother. You know they caught me before. They don't like me and they don't like Blacks.'

'They let you off the last time.'

'Now I have got a record they will never let me off.'

'Do you swear to the Lord Jesus Christ?'

'Yes, Mother, I do. That is what happened.'

She thought deeply. 'This time we must get a lawyer.'

'Who is going to pay for a lawyer? It's a waste of time and money. They will convict me anyway.'

'They cannot convict you if you are innocent, my son.'

'You are wrong. I wish you weren't but you are.'

'I will get you a good lawyer, Absolom. Master will help.'

'Don't ask the Whites for help, Mother—' The guard approached. The visit was over.

'I will get you free!' she shouted after him as he was led downstairs.

Poor Mary. She asked Robert on the evening after the wedding. She waited until Hazel was not around. She hoped that the sterling service she had provided during the wedding had been noticed, and that Robert would be sympathetic.

Robert was sitting in the lounge alone while Hazel was getting dressed for an evening at the theatre. He had indulged a little too much at the wedding, and still felt bloated.

Mary brought in a tray of drinks. 'Can I talk to you, Master?' she asked nervously.

'Yes, Mary?' He dreaded domestic drama.

'It's my son, Master.'

'Yes, of course. How is he getting on at school?'

'He is twenty-two, Master.' She spoke without resentment.

'I see.' He feels uncomfortable. But he can't be expected to know everything about the servants, can he? 'Very well, what is it?'

25

She tried to hold the tears back but they squeezed out. 'He – he needs a lawyer, Master.'

'What has he done?' Robert now knew that the interview would end with a request for money. This sort of interview always did.

'He has done nothing, Master. They *say* he stole some shoes.'

'And he didn't?' Robert went cold as he saw the tear sparkling down her cheek.

'No, Master.' Hands try to stop the tears escaping.

'Mary,' Hazel called from upstairs. 'Where is my red blouse? Mary!'

Robert whispers urgently, 'Stop it, Mary. I'm sure everything will be all right. You don't want her to see you like this.'

'Will you help me, Master?' she asked.

'Just wipe your face, I'll see what I can do.' He paraded potential sources of money through his head.

Four

We'll skip through the next few months. They were pulsating with drama, corny revelations – real life is usually corny – various family upheavals punctuating a glorious spring, then a sweltering summer.

Absolom was imprisoned for two years despite the efforts of Robert's lawyer, who had billed Robert as part of another transaction, thus keeping Hazel in the dark. To no avail. Absolom sat in a prison cell and learnt to grind his teeth.

The transaction in question was the sale of Robert and Hazel's house. To Hazel's horror, there was no other way to pay pressing bills. They had to move to a flat in a very smart block in Killarney which was just big enough for the two of them and the baby. Joseph and James were fired, but Mary was kept on and lived in a little room on the top floor of the block.

Anne and Daniel had to find somewhere else to go. They moved in with Aunt Erica (Anne's) whose husband had died a year ago. Auntie was a marvel. A radical feminist all her life (since long before those two words were married), she was a boozy, cackling mountain of fun, and seemed to be enjoying widowhood immensely. She reasoned that Michael, her 'Late' as she called him (because he always was, she said), had loved a good time himself and would have hated her being miserable. Fair do's, she said. (I could have told her otherwise.)

She used to go to the cemetery, silly woman, and whisper to the headstone. Years later I asked her what she whispered. 'I tell him dirty stories,' she confessed, with a blushing, girlish giggle.

When Anne became unwieldily fat as I grew relentlessly within her, they borrowed money from Auntie and the bank and bought a little house in Greenside.

Greenside was only just respectable, on the borders of the Pale. The house was pretty enough, with a trailing grapevine and a little half-acre garden. It had no swimming pool, and needed only two servants to run the whole place.

The two servants were the gardener, who called himself 'Sixpence' (because his real name was too difficult for stupid Whites to pronounce) and a lovely maid/cook – a niece of Mary Molapo, fresh from the country. Her name was Francine. She was little, shy and stunningly pretty. She lacked the attributes most black men prized – big tits 'n' bum. She was slim and leggy with the kind of figure most white men prized.

Suddenly one day Hazel gave birth. Everybody had secretly expected her to have a terrible time – her age, her nature, her shape. But in the event it was just a squat-plop affair. One day she was pregnant, the next a doctor went rushing to the flat to find that she and

27

Mary had performed everything necessary already. And a pink, yelling baby boy was making upside-down swimming motions on the coverlet. More of him later. My semi-step-uncle Anthony.

As the other baby (me) became less an unsightly bulge and more an impending person, Daniel began to make money at last. He changed from toys to furniture – manufacturing kitchen tables and chairs in a little factory in Germiston. As a result of cricket-club and war-buddy connections, he had managed to secure sizeable orders. The main problem was production.

One day there was a fire. I believe him when he says it was an accident; nevertheless, it provided insurance money, which enabled him to buy new machines and fulfil the growing order book.

My turn at last. I can delay the moment no more. The Official Opening of the Womb, the emergence into daylight of me, this life:

On the day I was born at the Brentwood Nursing Home ('Such a fuss! All that expense!' – Hazel) the late summer sun beamed at Daddy, who was playing cricket. At ten in the morning, when I poked my head out of that nice warm place inside my mother, Daniel was batting. He had scored twenty-two runs. He was caught out by Rosen. The score was 115 for 4. He felt sick as he walked back to the changing rooms, where Wilf stuck a cigar into his mouth. 'I only made twenty-two, you bastard,' said Father. 'You also made a son,' said Wilf.

Daniel ran out of the pavilion and drove at an illegal speed to the hospital. He parked the car dangerously on a kerb. He ran up the stairs to her ward. Mother said, 'Hallo, Father,' and he kissed her. When he saw me I said, 'Hallo, Father,' too but he didn't understand.

A Bris

I was quite unprepared for what came next. I had forgotten the perils of being born Jewish. I had forgotten that in order to be a proper Jewish male, I had to lose a portion of my dick. Unfortunately, the man who was to be directly responsible for my first traumatic experience had forgotten to be sober that morning.

I sit on a stranger's knee. Men in suits stand around chatting. It is becoming painfully clear to me that I'm about to be involved in an ancient rite. This is a rite I have never experienced before and I am fascinated.

The stranger is holding me awkwardly. None of my protests appear to have any effect, so I decide to try the Traditional Extended High-Pitched Squeal routine. The intention of this ploy is to make it impossible for adults to hear each other speak. This forces them to act.

The stranger shifts his grip. I am still not comfortable. I increase the volume and intensity of the squeal. To no avail. I try the next decibel level. All conversation stops. I have won, and am transferred to Father's kindlier lap.

I realise that the only way to communicate with adults is on a very basic level. Perhaps they do not understand Serbo-Croat. Perhaps my tongue and palate are not yet adapted to producing intelligible speech. I will have to train them.

I note with amusement that Robert is present. I wonder what *he* thinks of this Jewish ceremony. He certainly looks awkward in his borrowed Jewish togs.

A man dressed in black robes, wearing a striped white silk scarf, with a silly little cap on his head, and reeking of alcohol, bubbles and burps into the room.

'So this is the little boy,' he says, poking his many-folded face at me. 'What's his name?'

'Thomas,' says Daniel.

'Kootchie kootchie,' says the mohel trying to tickle me under the chin, which I resent and say so. He stares. His lips move as if to say something, then decide not to. I think he understood. He shakes his head as if to clear out cobwebs. 'Well,' he says, 'shall we begin?'

He opens a book and mutters unintelligible things in a sing-song voice. He opens a velvet bag containing a vicious little knife, some antiseptic, an ugly pliers-like instrument.

Hang on, I say. He stops praying and stares at me in confusion. 'What?' he whispers in Serbo-Croat. Everybody is staring.

'What's the matter, Mr Goldman?' Daniel asks, concerned, and frightened by the wafts of brandy-breath hovering over him.

'Nothing,' says the mohel and tries to carry on the ceremony. He picks the knife up and blesses it. I shout, What are you going to do with that? Again he stops dead, smothered in terror. He looks to my dad for help, confirmation that he's not hearing things. 'What did he say?' he whispers, pointing to me.

'What do you mean?' Daniel whispers back. Everyone is leaning forward, trying to make out what's happening.

'What's happening?' the mohel asks.

The others crowd around. 'Go on, man,' says Lionel.

The mohel stares at me as if I'm a ghost or a demon. He whispers in Serbo-Croat, 'If you are a devil and you understand me, shut up! Just shut up!'

I am thrilled. At last I have met someone who understands me. I immediately fall in love with the mohel and resolve to learn all about Judaism from him after the ceremony.

Suddenly he is holding my penis with his tongs. He starts to cut ... Forgetting everything but the pain I scream! I scream with the terror of castration that has haunted me in many of my male lives. I scream again, again. I swear at the mohel using all the bad words I can think of. His hand shakes horribly. The more I scream, the more his hand shakes. Blood sprays about the room. Then it is finished. And I have fainted. So has the mohel.

Thus did I carelessly lose my foreskin. I say carelessly because had I known about this idiotic custom, I would certainly not have been born Jewish.

I don't really remember whether things happened quite like that, or whether I recalled as much Serbo-Croat then as I do now. You must admit, though, if it did happen like that, it would have been very funny. The mohel would have stopped boozing for life. Or decided to booze himself to death.

As it was, he died of cirrhosis of the liver two years later.

Serves him right.

The episode is nevertheless very significant, for it saw the beginning of my distrust of people garbed in religion; it undermined any possibility of my being happily Jewish; it marked the beginning of my distrust of my father; and the commencement of all my sexual hang-ups.

Mary rocked little Anthony in her brown arms. She sang softly, 'Tula, tula wena . . .' Her eyes brimmed with tears. She wished she were holding her own son. The kitchen clock ticked slowly.

Hazel sat in the lounge reading a romantic novel. She too had tears in her eyes. She was weeping about the hero of the novel, a brave young man who had died on the fields of Flanders, leaving his girlfriend pregnant and destitute in her Mayfair flat.

Robert came into the room and threw his jacket on a chair. 'What's the matter?' he asked.

'Nothing – nothing, dear,' she said, sighing and

removing the salty tears which had spoiled her perfect make-up.

'Good, good.' Relieved that there were no new domestic dramas, he wondered why she called him Dear. 'How's Anthony?'

'Oh fine,' she said, laying the book down reluctantly. 'How was the service?'

'It wasn't actually a service,' he said. 'They call it a *Bris*. It was quite ghastly, actually.'

'I think it's barbaric,' she said.

He poured himself a drink and sat on the couch facing her. 'The child screamed horribly,' he said, sipping at the whisky. 'And you know, no one said anything to me at all.'

'That's strange.'

'Yes, it was,' he said with a little sigh. 'And I had to wear a hat.'

'I know,' she said, losing interest. She picked up the book and resumed her reading.

He watched her for a while. He had learnt not to resent the way she ignored him sometimes. He was still feeling shaken from the events at the Bris. He had found the bloody little operation harrowing.

'We're going to have to go on holiday,' he said.

Hazel put the book down.

One

PIETER DAWID MOSTERT was born on November 12th, 1948. His birth was a cause of dimay to at least two people. They were his half-sister Helena, two, and his half-brother Jakobus, four. Both were the products of their father's first marriage. Pieter was the issue of the second, which had occurred when their father, Japie, was forty-six years old.

Japie's second marriage had aroused much gossip at the time. The *oumas, oupas, tannies* and their ilk who ran the little farming village of Ventersdaal in the beautiful Eastern Transvaal couldn't work out what the drunken farmer saw in the ugly youngest daughter of their police chief.

Some expressed the hope that Hester Strijdom would reform the reprobate. Others pointed out that Hester liked a drop herself. Some knew the truth.

The village was a tidy place. It reeked of order. It was located in the bend of a river in the foothills of the dramatic Drakensberg Mountains, looking from the air like hairs in an armpit. Its people were mostly wealthy, churchgoing Afrikaners, attended by the massive entourage of Blacks the society needed to run the farms, the businesses and the white houses. The Blacks were mainly kept out of sight in their little huts on the farms or in the *pandokkies*, a group of tin huts, half-way up the hill.

One aspect of Japie's character which was not generally known amongst the white population – though it certainly was rumoured – was that Japie had a taste for black women, as well as for the potent beer they brewed. This aberration of his was, of course, known to almost the entire black population, many of whom did not hesitate to profit from it.

It was this 'flaw' in his character which resulted in his second marriage.

This was how it happened: The Chief of Police was interrogating a black man. In the course of the interrogation, the story of the clandestine night activities of the farmer came out. Captain Strijdom punished the black man for lying with a few strokes of the sjambok and decided that it was his duty to get to the bottom of the allegation. For the purpose of which he resolved that Japie would have to be caught in the act.

Captain Strijdom and Japie Mostert were old acquaintances. More than one complaint had been laid against Japie by various upstanding members of the Ventersdaal community. This was, however, the first opportunity the worthy Captain had of actually doing anything concrete about the village reprobate.

So the Captain planned a military-style operation to stake out the Mostert farm. (The Captain was a great fan of gangster movies and especially of Edward G. Robinson, whom he unconsciously imitated.) He placed his men in strategic positions around the farmhouse. This wasn't easy, as there was very little cover. His men were dressed in camouflage jackets, and had leaves and twigs sticking out of their hair. Luckily for the Captain, Japie was far too drunk to notice the wriggling bushes which had suddenly appeared in his backyard.

34

Mostert had spent the early part of the evening indulging in the time-honoured pursuit of drowning the memory of his dead wife in beer. The Afrikaans idiom which describes his condition translates roughly as 'He was high in the branches' or had 'looked too far into the bottle'. In English, Japie Mostert was pissed.

Finally at midnight (by which time half Strijdom's men were asleep, one third were suffering from chills and the remainder were bored out of their minds) Mostert staggered outside into the menacing dark. The lower buttons of his shirt had burst, and his hairy belly flopped out over his beer-stained trousers. He was singing as he went. The song was 'Sarie Marais', the old Boere lament, with only half-distinguishable but definitely disgusting new lyrics.

The Captain signalled the advance. Those of his men still awake tiptoed after him in single file.

A mad moon grinned. A dog barked. One of the stalkers tripped over a root and swore savagely. Mostert lumbered obliviously ahead of them, toward Big Selina, with her vast crushing tree-trunk arms, rotted teeth and excellent beer.

Like a crocodile at a party, the long line of men wove its way up the hill, toward the Pandokkies. The police stopped dead a few yards away as Strijdom signalled for them to halt. They picked themselves up from the ground and gathered around their leader. 'Gather round, men,' he said in his Edward G. voice. 'This is it!'

'What do we do now, Cappie?' Jannie DuPlessis whispered.

'Stay put, men,' said Strijdom. 'We gotta observe.'

The hut door opened. Mostert fell inside. On tiptoes the Captain crept to the window and crouched there, listening.

Suddenly his body stiffened and had there been more light, and had there been anyone watching him, they would have seen that brave stalwart of the South African Police go terribly pale.

'What's wrong, Cappie?' little Hennie Pieters asked in a hoarse whisper which must have carried three hundred yards.

'Shut your trap,' the Captain answered.

The men knew there was something horribly wrong. Unable to stay where they were, they trickled to the window like raindrops into a ditch and as they crouched there listening, they too began to pale and to wish they were anywhere else than there.

Because, from that glassless window, mixed with the giggles of willing black women and the sound of clattering mugs, there were many voices they recognised – apart from Japie's drunken growl. There was also the high-pitched laughter of Fanie De Jong, another prominent farmer. The throaty cries of protest of his brother, Hendrik, who was an elder of the church and local magistrate – and, worst of all, the drunken singing of Koos Pretorius, the dominee of the local Dutch Reformed Church.

While the forces of the law leaned over each other trying desperately to see into the smoky gloom, riddled with indecision, Japie's fate was being decided by forces totally outside anyone's control.

Let me introduce you to one of the least consequential characters in this entire history. His name is Kobus and his genus *Brakkie*. A brakkie is the sort of ragged starving little mongrel used by poor people all over the world to protect their property, keep festering food off the street and, no doubt, provide food themselves should that ever become necessary. Kobus was a brakkie of very little brain. Which made him unlikely to react to the intrusion of a mere gang of policemen with charcoaled faces and twigs in their hair in the same way that you, or I – were we canine in that particular life – would have done.

Kobus wandered sniffing round a corner of the shack, looking for food, or sex, or a place to leak. Unusual new smells and strange sounds assailed his twitching nose and ears. Suddenly he saw the minions of the law and let out a startled yelp which meant, 'What th' fuck!', followed by barks which meant, 'Get your filthy arses off my patch!' and 'Look out, chaps! Here come de fuzz!'

Frightened out of their wits by the racket, the lawmen hopped about in confusion. Their captain, however, reacted instantly to the threat as he had been taught in Police School. He drew his revolver and peppered the night with random shots.

If this were a war story the next sentence would be, All Hell Broke Loose. As it's not, let's say, There was Instant Bedlam. The other men, following the Captain's example, whipped their revolvers out of their holsters and let loose an unholy fusillade of shots in every direction. It is one of those peculiar miracles – and proof of my good nature – that Kobus escaped with nothing worse than a slightly shorter tail.

To the men inside the shack and the women who attended them the explosions seemed to be the sounds of their reputations shattering.

They tumbled out, pale and trembling, to face their terrible destinies. The two farmers, the reprobate and the respectable; the local Magistrate muttering, 'It's the Revolution.' And the Dominee, buttoning his shirt and clutching his trousers, throwing a quick prayer at God. They faced the police chief and his officers in the gibbering moonlight. The women huddled inside and screamed. One collapsed in hysterics. Kobus ran around in circles, trying desperately to identify and salve the burning sensation in his tail.

Strange to tell it was Japie who grasped the situation and decided on a course of action. 'Jan,' he said, addressing the police chief, 'why don't we go to my place and discuss all this?'

They trooped down to the farm. The only sound was the shuffling of feet.

It was a long night. At first Strijdom was adamant.

He felt very powerful, sitting in Mostert's living room, dangling the fates of the town's most prominent citizens before them. However, as the beer flowed (Mostert was smart enough to realise that the best way to defuse the situation was with alcohol), the Captain's resolve to prosecute was eroded away. The advantages of a 'civilised agreement' (as the Dominee called it) became clearer as the offers from the farmers, magistrate and preacher grew more extravagant.

Finally, at about five in the morning, the police staggered out of Mostert's house, some singing, others leaning on their comrades, one being violently sick. Each was seraphic. For each had twenty pounds in cash in his pocket. The Captain chortled about his promised new car, his fifty acres of land, his antique Bible and – most important – the paper of agreement in which Japie agreed to marry his eldest, fattest and ugliest daughter, Hester.

The advantages of the match were immense. For Jan Strijdom, anyway. For one thing, no one else would voluntarily have married his daughter. For another, he now had an interest in one of the richest farms in the valley. And best of all, a spy in the enemy camp.

(A rider: Funnily enough, Japie fell deeply in love with Hester. Like him, she had been rejected and scorned all her life. Like him, she regarded all men as fools. Like him, she had a healthy hatred of the law and a love of drink. Furthermore she was fat, and as we have already seen, Japie liked fat women. He stayed faithful to her for the rest of his life. As for *her* – well that's another story.)

The aforegoing is based on a true event that happened in the Orange Free State, where the outcome for the town notables was not half so happy.

Two

Ventersdaal Skool was sunken in sunlight. The almost solid sunbeam came pouring into the room where it ate the darkness. Pieter sat at his desk staring into the sunbeam.

He picked his turned-up nose abstractedly and wiped the bogies under the desk where they contributed to a vast and growing colony of snot. Outside dogs barked and Blacks chattered. Occasionally a motor car coughed past. The English composition he was supposed to be writing was stuck at the words: My Holiday. 'I didn't go on holoday this years becars I was sick.'

He couldn't think of anything else to write. Even the first sentence was a lie. He had never had a holiday. Not because his parents couldn't afford it; they just didn't seem interested. Both his brother and sister had been on a school trip to the Kruger National Park to see the animals, but they were 'old enough' and his parents always considered him too young for anything.

Pieter was in no hurry to finish the composition. Outside legions of boys, probably led by his half-brother, would be waiting to get him. To shove mud down his trousers. To humiliate him in any one of the thousands of ways children can dream up.

He sniffed. He knew that old Bones (the teacher) had kept him after school out of sympathy and a desire to protect him. He was grateful. He was angry. It was a perpetual motion machine – his schoolfellows bullied him, so the teachers protected him, so the kids bullied him more.

He turned his attention again to the expanse of striped white paper on the desk and screwed up his eyes, desperately trying to conjure English words out of the air. Without success. He could go on lying. He could write about a holiday Jannie Pretorius had described to him. A holiday in Durban where stunningly white beaches were spattered with rich ladies in shocking bikinis. But the words wouldn't come.

Pieter shut his eyes and tried to imagine Durban. He dreamed of escape. Of freedom.

Why *shouldn't* he escape? Once again the old dream of running away had returned. And this time it grew.

Carefully he wrote in English: 'I am now running away. Good Bye.' He stared at the words, shining briefly as they dried. Permanent. Stuck there on the page. Impossible to remove.

He looked up and noted that Bones was asleep at his desk. As usual.

He tiptoed to the window. Squinting into the sun, he searched what he could see of the playground. There was no one in sight. He hopped lightly out of the window, clutching his satchel which contained a half-eaten sandwich, an English grammar, and his collection of semi-precious stones.

He rounded a corner of the school. To be grasped by the coat.

'Teacher has let the monkey out, hey?' It was Jakobus, his dreaded elder half-brother, the person Pieter hated as fiercely as anyone could hate anyone.

Pieter struggled furiously. 'Let me GO!' he shouted.

Jakobus was delighted with his catch. 'Where do you think you're going, you little squirt?' He turned to a group of boys playing a lazy game of marbles in the sun and yelled, 'Come and see the monkey I've caught!'

A blaze of black and red obscured Pieter's vision. He swung the satchel savagely. It hit Jakobus's head with a crunching sound.

His brother let go of his jacket and slumped against the wall. Blood ran down his face.

Pieter screamed. Then, clutching the satchel he ran, little legs whirring through the dust of the sleepy village.

Three

I wasn't too popular at school either. Well, primary school was OK, but the minute I got to high school the trouble began.

To say that I was victimised would be an understatement. It would not convey the viciousness of which the scions of the rich and nearly rich are capable.

Back to Pieter, running for his life, the murder weapon clutched in grubby hands. Cain and Abel, he kept thinking.

Cain and Abel!

He would go into the wilderness. He would hide. He would wait for the terrible summons of God.

As his breathing became harder he had to concentrate on not slipping on the green slopes of the hill. His head began to clear. He realised that he didn't feel guilty. After all, if he *had* killed Jakobus, he had rid the world of a burden, a pest, a loathsome mouther of obscenities, the source of all his pain.

Exhausted, he collapsed on a bush-strewn outcrop of rock. He could see the village dozing in the heat. The Scene of the Crime. He expected to see police and dogs appear any minute but the village stayed innocently asleep.

Head on hands, legs drawn up in the foetal position, Pieter sat there till sunset.

Then he got up and set off on his pilgrimage. Visions of jumping on to a ship bound for – India? the East? But Pa said those Indians were no better than the Blacks. Ma said they had an older civilisation than us. Pa said that's why they were so backward. Second childhood.

If he went to America he could be a cowboy. 'Wal mam ah got no passt but we sure as hell gonna have us a future!' he muttered, caressing an imaginary six-gun.

In the red glow of the departing sun, he saw a small group of huts ahead. Rusting, corrugated iron, supported by beams and sticks, a scrawny dog nosing around bags of rubbish. (This was the grandson of brave Kobus, whose fault Pieter was.) By now you will have guessed that Pieter was visiting those same *Pandokkies* his father used to visit. Long ago.

Pieter was conscious of only one overwhelming sense-impression. The clinging, passionate odour of grilling meat.

No amount of indoctrination, of Bones's warnings could have severed the invisible chord between Pieter's stomach and the source of that titillating smell.

Pieter went to the single-hinged door and knocked.

The date, by the way, was March 21st, 1960.

Earlier on this autumn day, Absolom Molapo and other Pan African Congress members were in the little township of Sharpeville, organising a demonstration. The demonstration was aimed at the hated pass laws, which require black people to carry a little book which says who they are, where they work, where they are allowed to be.

There were schoolchildren, students, old folks, then there were police and then there were sixty-nine people dead.

Pieter wolfed down a bowl of mealiepap and meat, the provenance of which we had best not go into, not that the boy would have minded. Selina fussed over him blowsily, her sweat-stained dress desperately trying to hold her together and prevent her flowing out all over the floor. Even the rheumatism in her joints didn't affect the flow of her rampant good humour. 'Ah,' she exploded, *'what* am I going to do with you!' She slapped him on the back, nearly causing his frantic young life to exit via his throat – though not causing a pause in his attempts to shovel all the food in in one go.

'Ai, sistog, he's *such* a tsotsi! Are you going to eat the plate as well?'

Pieter sputtered, *'Please* don't send me home, Selina!' and carried on eating.

'And what if I don't send the little tsotsi home? His big father will come and shoot us all, that's what his big father will do. They will say the Blacks kidnapped you. That's what they will say. Au, you want more? You will eat us all to death!' Her pretended dismay belied by her eyes and the huge second helping she piled on to his plate.

Pieter slowed. He was feeling nicely bloated at last. He couldn't decide whether to eat or cry. He decided on a mixture of both. Soggy porridge.

'Please don't send me home,' he tried again.

She whooped. 'And what is home to you, boy? That nest of Mosterts! *Why* don't you want to go home? *What* have you done?'

'Nothing, Selina, really. I have to go to America, to be a cowboy.'

'Oh yes. So you are going to be a cowboy. And *who* is going to iron your shirts? Just tell me that. Who is going to make your dinner? I'm sure they don't eat properly oversea.'

'They don't need servants over there, Selina. They do everything themselves. Or maybe the Indians do it.' He was imparting facts guessed from Westerns.

'Pieter, *I brought you up.* What good is oversea? All they got there is big buildings. What you going to do in all those big buildings?'

This portrait of Selina is true. Blacks on farms in South Africa hardly ever saw movies. Most of them were illiterate. Still are. Their knowledge of the outside world was scanty, gained mainly from hearsay. There was as yet no television in South Africa – Pieter, me, Absolom, all the characters in this book grew up without ever seeing *Blue Peter,* or *John Craven's News-round.* There were the movies, of course, but that's hardly the same thing. So most rural Blacks imagined that Apartheid was a universal condition. Perhaps it is.

'And *who* will iron your shirts?' Selina said again, almost tearfully.

Don't laugh at Selina. She really loved the boy. She never saw her own son who had gone off to work and scrounge amongst the dustbins in Soweto. She had changed Pieter's nappies when he was a baby. She had cleaned the shit lovingly from his bottom. She had dodged blows from his mother who had always found something to complain about when she was drunk. She was usually drunk. Now Selina was exiled to the Pandokkies because her health was failing and she was costing the Mosterts too much in medical bills.

From Pa Mostert's Bit of Black to servant to cast-off. All those years she had loved Pa Mostert too. Hated his wife. Loved his child.

Selina waxed weepy. 'He wants to go oversea, my big boy, he wants to leave his Selina and go away!' Her joy at seeing the child had evaporated. She realised that it was getting late. He was eating more slowly now. When the plate was empty he would have to do something. And she would have to do something.

Selina made a decision. 'You stay here,' she commanded, and left.

Pieter stopped eating, pushed the plate away, leaned back. He felt safe here, though it *was* getting chilly. . .

He shivered. Night was closing in. Pa would be looking for him. Pa and his sjambok. Ma would be nagging the servants. Perhaps the police were combing the hillside even now, with dogs.

The door creaked open, swinging crazily on its single hinge. An old, old man slid in, mud crackling into dust on his ragged clothes. Pieter jumped up in sudden fright. The skull face was topped by scarce skrawls of white white hair. Skin seemed to flake off at every moment, as if he had dandruff all over.

44

'Sit down, little one,' he said in Afrikaans. 'So you are run away?'

'Who are you?' Pieter asked, keeping as far away as the wall of the shack allowed.

'I am Umfaan. Sit down. You and I are going to have a talk.'

Pieter sat. '*Umfaan* means "boy", doesn't it?'

'All Blacks are "boy" to you, aren't they, Pieter Mostert? However old, however educated, however dignified?'

A memory stirs in Pieter's mind. 'Are you a Comminis?' he asked, agape.

'You don't know what a Communist is, do you? No. I am not a Communist. I am a man. I am called "boy". Where are you going to run to?'

To Pieter this man seems like a devil. He has never met such an articulate, unrespectful black man. He answers bewitched. 'I have to go away. I will become a cowboy.'

The old man laughed like a bird being run over by a lawn-spike. 'So you want to be a cowboy! Oh, it is too much. I have been a cowboy myself,' he said, suddenly becoming serious. 'Yes, in 1892.'

'*Were* you?' Pieter was intrigued. 'Are there black cowboys?'

'Oh yes, of course there are. Who do you think irons the cowboys' shirts?' He doubled up with laughter for a while, then, as before, he switched to instant seriousness. 'Tell me Pieter, did you ever hear about Doc Halliday, and the OK Corral?'

'Were *you* there?'

'Me there? Of course! I will tell you about it. Do you want to hear?'

The boy's eyes widened. He pushed the food bowl out of the way and leaned forward on the table.

The old man began.

How the Blacks Won the West

'Well, when I was a cowboy way back in the far time of the Old West, I was one of a bunch of Blacks – the ones you never hear about, the ones you won't find in Zane Grey – the ones who used to iron the shirts, make the beans, clean the guns and shine the boots.

'You didn't know about that, did you? And the other great secret which no movie will show you, no comic book will explain is that when it came to the shooting, it was the Blacks, dressed as their white masters, who went out and banged away at each other.'

Pieter giggled, unbelieving.

'No, don't look like that. You must believe everything I say, because I am Umfaan. But the guns were always filled with blanks, see, and the Whites would watch and decide who was the winner. Then the master of the Black who was declared the loser would have to go off into the bush and shoot himself, after of course shooting his servant as a punishment for losing.

'It became a tradition, after a while, for the losing master not to shoot himself but instead to run off, black up his face, bang a shot into the air so the others would think he was dead, and become a servant to someone else for a while. Then if *his* master won the next fight, he would kill him and take his place.

'Well, as you can imagine, this became so complicated that after a few years, everybody forgot who was black and who was white and who was to shoot who when. This is the reason everybody forgets to mention the black folk – who, if the truth were known, were the ones who truly won the West.'

'Gosh,' Pieter said, thinking, What nonsense, anybody could easily have worked out who was black and who was white! The whites were the *clever* ones, weren't they? 'Tell me about the OK Corral now.'

The old man laughed. 'Young people. Always hurry hurry. All right. I was the servant of the man they called Doc Halliday and to be honest with you, I was so old, I had long ago forgotten if I was black or white and so had my master.

'Anyway, if you have read your history, you know that the OK Corral was where the famous bandit Roy Rogers met his Trigger, and Doc Halliday and Wyatt Earp had them surrounded.

'It was devilishly hot on that afternoon. As agreed, on the stroke of four o'clock, the combatants met in the Corral. First, they sent in their servants, including me, to empty the place of the horses, cows and sheep and while we did that, they discussed what was going to happen.

' "Wal," Wyatt said, "first, we gotta decide who's Good and who's Bad, right?"

' "Right," said Trigger. "Wal, ah want to be a Goody this time. Ah'm sick of bein' shot up."

'Roy Rogers stamped his foot. "Fergit it," he said. "*First* decide who's gonna win. *Then* we can consider whut side to take, right?" I must explain that these two were deeply in love and always did everything together.

' "Wal, you all better deecide goddamn quick, because I gotta deecide which of you ah'm gonna patch up after," said the Doc.

' "You all always damn arguin'. What's the difference anyway, the Blacks are gonna git it," said Wyatt.

'Well, those guys went on arguing with each other like this for a long long time and we had already done *our* part of the job. We Blacks stood there, waiting for them to make up their minds, waiting to get their clothes and guns so we could get on with the shooting.

'And when it got to time for the sun to set, we were very bored. So I said, "Look, why don't you stop all this arguing? I've got the best idea how to sort all this out."

47

' "Oh yeah?" said Trigger. "So what's a smartass Black gonna do about it?"

' "Give me your gun," I said, and he handed it over.

'The Whites stood about laughing, and I let them have it. Six bullets in the Colt, four men dead and two bullets left.

' "Au!" said the other servants, "what you do that for? Now we are really in trouble!" '

Pieter laughed, incredulously. 'And then what did you do, Umfaan?' he asked.

'Obvious! We took the guns off the dead Whites, and rode off into the sunset. Unfortunately, we were soon caught in an ambush by the servants of a posse sent to find us. There was a great shooting match and me the only one who lived to tell the tale.'

'Gosh,' said the boy.

'Now I have to tell you something else,' the old man whispered, 'and this is something very special between you and me.'

The boy leaned forward.

'In a few minutes your father will be here with his sjambok.'

The boy jumped up in terror. 'Where? You've been keeping me here—' He felt desperate, betrayed.

'Wait! You are here for a reason.' He grabbed Pieter by the shoulder and held him with great strength. 'This is your fate. You came here because you had to meet me. This was your fate. Your father will take you home. He will whip you until you see blue.'

'Let me go!'

'You have not killed your brother. He is bruised and angry, but he is not dead. From now on he will respect you, perhaps he will stop tormenting you.'

'How did you know about that?'

'I know everything. If you come again, and you will come again, I will teach you many things.'

The terrified boy squirmed, trying to bite the hand that grasped him like an iron claw.

Pa Mostert stormed in like the Old West. The old man grinned so that his face became a devilish road-map. 'Here he is, baas,' he said. 'Waiting for you.'

Four

Absolom Molapo sat on his mother's bed. He wore torn and dirt-streaked clothes. He shook uncontrollably. Mary sat in the plastic chair facing him. Both mother and son had aged considerably in the last few years. Absolom had aged horrifically in the last few hours.

'It was the pass laws, my mother, that we demonstrated against. Why should we all be marked men? Why *should* we be treated like shit always? Are we like the Jews who were fed to the furnaces like dead logs?'

'Hush, Absolom. Tell me what happened then.'

'I burned my pass. They were all there, the PAC. But there were also – I don't know how many thousand other people, ordinary people, they had come there to burn their passes too.'

'You have burned your pass? What are you going to do?'

'The pass is the symbol of our oppression, Mama. If I carry one it burns my pocket.'

'What happened then, Absolom?'

'The police came and told us to disperse. We did not disperse.'

'Oh God.'

'Then they opened *fire*, Mother, they shot at all the people. Women and children died as well as the men. I *carried* a little boy who had been hit. I just picked him up and ran with him. I hid behind a hut. He stopped breathing. I was so full of shock. I hugged that boy to me. I shook him as if that would make him live. I could not give him even a little of this life I have.' Finally

49

Absolom cried, wrackingly, the release he needed coming at last to him here in the safe arms of his mother.

Absolom Molapo was thirteen when he joined the ANC. The boy who died in his arms was thirteen too. For years – even while he was still at school – Absolom ran errands for the ANC, distributing leaflets, dodging police, trying to give the black people a message of hope via the vehicle of anger. He had been arrested many times. His body bore the scars of many interrogations.

'You will stay here until the fuss dies down,' Mary said. 'I will keep you very secretly.'

When Sharpeville happened, Mary wasn't too well herself. She tottered on unsteady swollen legs between her room and the kitchen of the Stones' flat. She prepared meals which were barely edible. She made shaky token gestures at the dust which led a generally happy life on Hazel's stinkwood, yellowwood and Imbuia furniture.

Hazel and Robert kept her on because she was cheap. Of course they espoused other reasons. 'She couldn't live without us,' Hazel would say, without having any idea that this was true.

Of course, the little family of three couldn't have survived without her either.

Hazel hated housework, but she also hated dirt. Since the accident, the Stones had been in Dire Financial Straits.

The Accident. I haven't told you about the Accident.

To tell you about it, back we go to 1948. Shortly after Anthony's birth, Robert decided to take his little family on a holiday to Durban.

O white folks' holidays! Days before, the servants start hard-boiling eggs, packing cases, repacking cases, servicing cars, piling stacks of sweet-smelling beach-towels, newly washed and ironed, into boxes.

Then, on the preceding day, a mass of sandwiches, bottles of Cola, cooked chicken, tomatoes, paper plates are packed tightly into a picnic basket. Comics are put in for the kids. Bottles of barley-sugars are brought along for the driver.

The excited little party is almost ready. The day of the trip dawns. At five in the morning Mommy supervises the loading of the limo. It creaks on its old springs and sinks inch by inch as each load is fussed in. By six, Mommy has had her suitcase out three times to check she has the red dress, or has packed the parasol, and how many handbags she has along.

At last! Six-thirty, just getting light. Daddy has had another cup of coffee, and the thermos is in the car. Daddy is going to drive because it's bad enough having to take Mary to nurse the baby without having to pay for the accommodation of a driver as well. Mommy gets in next to Daddy. Mary and the baby go into the back along with a mountain of ironed nappies; bottles; milk; towels; jars of babyfood, enough to feed six babies for twelve days. The petrol tank is full. The oil and water have been checked. The car gleams in the sunlight: a perfectly groomed antique, like Barbara Cartland or the Queen Mother. The baby wakes and starts whingeing and crying. Robert turns the radio on. Mommy and Daddy smile at each other. Worries lift. A holiday! A temporary halt in the ruthless advance of Fate!

'My little darling is crying. Shut him up, Mary.'

'Yes, madam.' Mary rocks little Anthony, prises his unwilling mouth open, forces mashed substances in.

Anthony was not a happy child. He had entered this life most reluctantly. He naturally resented his severance from a lush boudoir life in eighteenth-century France, where he had been the mistress of the Comte Lisle de Saint-Ferry. His – or should I say, her – life was summarily ended by Madame La Guillotine in 1792.

He grew up supercilious and arrogant. His attitude to me was one of affectionate contempt. Well, he was my

51

uncle. My Wicked Uncle. And he thought I didn't know that once, in one of my many incarnations, I had inhabited the fat, powdered body of the Comte Lisle de Saint-Ferry.

Back to the Holiday. By now the happy little quartet is winding its way through the madcap scenery of the Valley of a Thousand Hills. They are all a little faded, and even Anthony has stopped protesting in half-articulated French, about the discomforts of the journey. He and Mary sleep and dream of different things.

The road winds without any logic amongst some of the most beautiful views in the world. Hills, valleys – green, deep, spotted with flowers, sheep, huts like brown overgrown beehives. Robert is driving in a happy stupor. He feels the way the paterfamilias of an ideal family should feel.

Hazel spies something. 'Oh *look*, Robert!' she shouts excitedly.

Robert, startled, jerks round. The steering wheel jerks with him. The car flies majestically over the edge of the road, sails through the air in slow motion and then, fifty feet later, kisses earth.

For the car, kiss of death. For Hazel, a broken arm and a cracked rib. For Mary and the baby, minor bruising, for they were both asleep and Mary's soft body protected the child. For Robert, a journey through the windscreen.

And brain damage.

Well, nothing catastrophic. In fact, the doctors assured Hazel that there was no permanent damage. Rubbish! Robert's long-term memory was gone for good. He now fell asleep all the time, became irritable for no reason. No permanent damage! Rot.

Hazel had to take on the business. Robert was reduced to no more than a genial barman in Stones'. Hazel did the books, ordered the food, ran the staff, and ran the house. They struggled on.

And, after the accident, Hazel and Anthony fell more

52

deeply in love than ever – perhaps because she had come so close to losing him. They were obsessed with each other: a vampiric passion, riddled with jealousy.

By the way, do you want to know what attracted Hazel's notice and shattered their lives? Well, it was a large curiously man-shaped stone by the side of the road. Some idiot had painted clothes and a grinning face on the thing. Hazel thought it was funny and wanted Robert to look. That's all.

The day of Sharpeville wasn't too happy for me, either. During break I had been herded into a corner by a group of yowling boys. It is painful to me to write this. They teased me mercilessly, calling me a sissy and a variety of girls' names. Perhaps teasing me reassured them of their masculinity: that way they could hide from the guilt aroused by their experiments with sex in the dorm after dark. Scrawny, only too obviously vulnerable, I was a day-boy, and fair game.

My own sexual education, mainly in the hands (literally) of other boys my age, was proceeding at a frantic pace. Anthony, my cousin Julian, and a couple of others would have enthralling encounters on the roof of my parents' house. (By then Anne and Daniel had moved to Houghton in the salubrious and respectable Northern Suburbs of Johannesburg.) We called the game 'Cavemen'. We knew cavemen didn't wear any clothes and what more natural than that their normal form of greeting would be to rub their dicks together?

We did have one iron rule, though. No one was allowed to *come* – because that would be a *moffie* (Afrikaans slang, meaning 'queer', I suppose) thing to do. Perverted!

In the lower school I had been quite popular. What had gone wrong? How had I changed? I used to organise a

53

game of 'Catches' at break times, of which I was the self-appointed leader. The only rules of the game were, one: as leader I could not be caught, two: I made all the rules.

And I became pretty good at the bullying game myself. There was one boy called David who had good cause to hate me. It was so easy to be nasty. The challenge was to drive him to tears.

One day David caught me behind the school. He grabbed me by the collar. I remember thinking, I deserve this. I went completely limp. No resistance. He banged my head against the wall again and again. The Headmaster came out of his office and caught us in this passionate game of revenge and submission. When he asked what it was about, I refused to speak and so did David. He whacked us both soundly. Though I felt it was deserved, I resented David's punishment.

(David subsequently became my best friend, until we both left and went on to different schools. Many years later my parents sent me a press-cutting. Which said that he had got himself up on the roof of the Israeli Embassy in Johannesburg and, with a dummy machine-gun, had held off a vast battalion of police. Until they managed to gun him down. This story is true.)

What changed me? What caused me to metamorphose back from bully into bullied?

From the moment I walked through the gates of the King George V High School I felt oppressed, out of place like a speck of dust in a sore eye. The red-brick school buildings, sixty years old, the bricks almost luminous with the sweat, snot and blood of six hundred and fifty spoilt, sex-obsessed young men. The urinals always stank in that school. From yards away. The rugby posts aggressively giving the finger to God. The desks whittled to the bone with initials and obscene and mysterious messages. The boys with their jagged short-back-and-sides, their long grey shorts,

54

their dust-stained green blazers, their frayed-hem white shirts.

A colour photograph of the school would have been quite beautiful. Oak trees, ivy-coloured buildings. Every cliché there in splendour. A fair attempt at imitating academe.

The reality was cruelly different. Or so it seemed to me. Within those august walls schemes were schemed, plots were plotted and everyone lived their little boxed lives as if the school were the whole world.

And we, the crisply laundered sons of the rich were supposed to learn – about the world? – in this claustrophobic, distorted imitation of real life.

From deranged and ragged men like old Matchstick, who was liable at any moment to leap on his chair screaming, 'I can't stand it! I JUST CAN'T STAND IT!' if a boy were, say, to pop a paper bag. Needless to say, popping paper bags was a popular sport among the apprentice sadists of the class. They say he was shell-shocked from the Great War. I say he was shell-shocked from being born. A strange experience, being born.

Other masters and mistresses all had their secret foibles. Brandie, the Latin master, a frenetic being with eyes that shot poison like a puff-adder at all but the Golden Boys – and especially at me. But then, he may have had good reason. We will come to that.

Gordie the Red, a furious freckled Scot, who gave up trying to teach me maths when I persisted in writing an Infinity sign 00 at the end of each sum. (All numbers end in Infinity, don't they, sir?) The Incredible Mistress Foxx who taught science: a mountainous woman, who could blow the brain of a naughty boy from one side of his head to the other with one resounding cuff to the ear.

There were one or two humans among them. Like the delicious Madame Bella, beloved by Schilbey (and most of her pupils) for her swinging tits and auburn hair. Fantasy fuel. Schilbey, the English master, was beloved by us too, because he spoke to us as if we were human beings. This pretty pair were always exploding, accusations of infidelity mostly. Occasionally these bombs went off in front of us. On one occasion, after she had slammed out of the class, Schilbey turned to us with a conspiratorial grin and said, 'Now boys, it's time I taught you the *proper* usage of the word "fuck".' He then gave us a lecture on the difference between 'fucking', 'making love' and 'having sex'.

The only person I really hated like cold porridge – or like Father – more than I hated the boys who ragged me and called me names, or the foolish teachers who tried to protect me, was the Head. The Hated Head. A rake of a man, muscles of string, bones of iron. Eyes sizzling with controlled malevolence. I hate him still, though he's dead, poor fellow. And he hated me. This is why:

In my fourth year at high school, I was appointed Editor of the school newspaper *Vigah*. Gosh. Traditionally dull, filled with sports results, old boy lectures about truth and beauty and Being Good, mostly rubbish really. Usual sale was about two hundred copies.

I decided to change all that.

I introduced short stories, competitions, reviews of school plays. Lennie and I were the entire staff of the paper, but that did not stop us writing numerous articles under fictional bylines. Our competitions were a hoot. One of the greatest scams was a 'Spot the deliberate typo' Competition. This was my brilliant response to the carping of English teachers at the vast numbers of errors our faulty, two-fingered typing caused. So we offered a prize to the boy who could identify them all. The prize was an astonishing £100. This aroused massive interest. Needless to say, the competition was fixed. There was always some grubby little swot in the Lower School who would gratefully accept £5 to be declared the winner.

56

The Short Story Competition was the best. In that the winning story was always written by me, and, once more, we could always find somebody who would accept the glory of winning without, necessarily, wanting the money as well.

The thing that caused me to run foul of the Head and made Brandie my worst enema (deliberate typo) was my review of the school play, which Brandie had produced. The play was Shaw's *Androcles and the Lion*, and my review might well be construed as sour grapes, since I had been awarded the part of a slave. Convinced that I was the greatest undiscovered talent in the school, I had naturally expected the part of Androcles.

The review simply said, '. . . isn't it amazing how the same boys get the good parts play after play . . .'

Under normal circumstances, an uncontroversial statement. Under the rather special circumstances prevailing – the Golden Boys always got the good parts, which turned the phrase into an accusation of homosexual behaviour – it was scandalous.

Brandie in tears. Me summoned by Headmaster. Secret convocations in the Bloch household, the Head occupying my father's favourite chair, I cowering by the footstool. ('Your boy is a disgrace to the school . . . Persistently disobedient . . . Give me one good reason for not expelling him.' And Father: 'Did you *want* my Company's grant for that Sports Scholarship?')

The most he could do was absolve us of our guilt by caning Lennie and me heartily, six of the best. It occurs to me that in those days of barbaric capital punishment, masters must have been extremely fit.

But then that was how they gave us our education. They beat it in with canes, shot it in with the hypodermic of their frayed wits, packed it up our arses with nearly sexual passion.

There were one or two gentle ones. They are the ones I've forgotten. It is far easier to remember the pain.

So the boys were riddled with sadism and anger,

which they could only express by bullying someone unable to resist. Me.

I could almost forgive them. I could certainly forgive Garry, who once whispered hoarsely to me in the library, 'I bet you've never *come*. I bet you've never felt a hot gob of spunk hitting your chest, right up to the tits, man!' He was one of my greatest tormentors. Dark and smouldering, full of passion. I must have loved him.

The other boys are a smudge of teeth and eyes, mocking teeth and eyes, leering mouths and mocking eyes. I have to decide whether to forgive them.

Seven years of that.

Four weeks after Sharpeville Absolom was grassed. It happened like this:

Hazel, Robert, Anthony sat in the living room. Hazel and Anthony hand in hand on the couch, Robert in his traditional chair by the desk. They looked as if they were posing for a Victorian photograph.

Green flocked wallpaper stared down. Paintings of Venice in elaborate frames with the gilding wearing off leaned away from the wall showing off to the carpet. The electric fire glowed to itself.

William the porter stood awkwardly in the middle of the room. He said, 'I am truly very sorry to have to tell you this and to interrup' your evening, madam.'

He spoke exclusively to Hazel. He had long realised that Boss Robert was incapable of maintaining an attention-span of longer than a minute.

'What is it, William?' Robert said, trying to be interested.

'Shut up, dear,' said Hazel. 'Go on, boy.'

'Yes, madam.' William was six foot seven, sixty years old. His shirt collar was black. His sleeves were frayed. His brown porter's uniform though grubby, was perfectly pressed. He carried a knobkerrie.

Sweat burst out of nervous pores under his arms, on his back, on his forehead. He loved his job. He swelled with self-importance when he was with other Blacks. He shrank with fear when in the presence of the white tenants on the block. He considered it his duty to protect them and guard them against a violent and uncertain world.

'Your maid, Mary Molapo, do you know she is keeping a man in her room?'

Robert laughed. 'I would have thought she'd be too old for that sort of thing.'

'Don't be *silly*, Robert. Who is this man?' Hazel checks Anthony's reactions.

'I think he is a big agitator, madam. From the ANC.'

'That's terrible,' Anthony said. 'Is it Mandela?'

'Ssh, darling, let me handle this. What is his name, William?'

'I don't know, madam.'

'Have the police been told?' Anthony asked.

Hazel twinkled with pride. As usual, her son had gone straight to the heart of the matter.

'No, Baasie. I wanted to tell the Madam first.'

'I think we should phone the police,' said Anthony.

'I don't know, dear, Mary is very faithful and we don't—'

Robert shook himself out of his torpor. His dented brain had found a part of itself that still worked. It ground into action like a restored antique steam-engine. 'No. I will go and talk to her.' He stood, stepped toward the door.

'Robert, sit down,' said Hazel.

'No,' he said. 'You must let me handle this.'

Was Robert inspired by pity? Was he exerting his long-abdicated rights as Head of the Family?

Hazel stood, draped a powerful arm around him, tried to force him to sit. Anthony said, as if to a dog, 'Sit, Daddy!' William was secretly amused.

'I will NOT sit!' He shook her arm from his shoulder.

Robert stood proud, lion of the roost, cock of the hoop. 'Take me to her room.'

The terrified William could only obey. Robert's wife and son stood speechless as if slapped across their faces.

Robert mounted the stairs with the dumbstruck William. The servants' quarters spread across the top floor of the building like a row of third-class railway carriages. A gently biodegrading contrast to the smart flats below. Rubbish lay about. The smell of dagga. 'Room 15, master,' said the porter.

Robert paused before the door, trying to decide whether to knock.

Then he forgot why he was there. Then he remembered. 'Are you going in?' asked William smugly.

'Of course I'm going in.' He knocked and opened the door immediately. The tableau inside: Mary on the chair, Absolom sitting on the bed, eating a bowl of mealiepap and meat. Frozen. Mary stood. 'Oh, master!'

'Mary, who is this man? Why are you keeping a man in your room?'

'Oh, master, please don't be angry—'

'Mary, answer me!'

Absolom put the bowl of food on the bed. Slowly, he stood up. He looked, in the dark, like a huge alien which was still growing and would continue to grow. 'Don't worry, Mama. I am her son, master.' Absolom automatically reverted to the accepted Master/Black behaviour. Eyes lowered, shuffling feet, suppressed fury.

Robert's anger swung around in a huge circle, collapsed in upon itself.

'Your son? Mary, I'm sorry—'

A crowd materialised in the room. Hazel, William, Anthony. William spoke, determined to prove that his actions had been correct. 'This man is a Communist, master. I know him. He is one of those ANC.'

Hazel reinforced William. 'He's a *Communist*, Robert.

Why don't you listen to the man?'

'Should I get the police?' from Anthony.

Robert saw his power crumbling, back-tracked. 'Be quiet, boy.'

'Don't tell him to be quiet,' Hazel whispered hoarsely.

'She is not allowed to have men in her room, master,' William added helpfully. 'Besides he's been here for weeks.'

'Please, master,' Mary said. She was sobbing.

'Are you a Communist, boy?' Robert asked Absolom.

'I am not.' Absolom look up, met his eyes, a meeting of equals.

Robert turned to the trio. 'He's not a Communist,' he told his family.

'That doesn't matter,' Anthony informed him. 'He's not allowed.'

'I didn't ask you.' Robert's suppressed resentment bubbled out. Let's face it, he was jealous. The attention Hazel lavished on Anthony instead of on him. He secretly hated the precocious pimpled adolescent.

'Don't talk to him like that – in front of the *servants*—'

'Don't you dare tell me what to do in my own house!' he thundered.

'I'm going to get the police,' the brat retorted. 'Anyway, this isn't your house.'

'I'll get you, you twerp!' Robert swung at Anthony whose little legs whirred him off at an Olympic rate.

Hazel screamed. 'I don't believe this! I don't believe this is happening!' Then, smothered in shame and anger, she followed her darling son.

William stared dumbly – at the remaining silent drama. Then, shouldering his knobkerrie, he decided to pretend that none of this had ever happened, and left, shaking his head.

Robert stood there in shock. 'You're not a Communist,' he stated.

'No, Mr Stone, I am not a Communist. I am very sorry to cause you this trouble.'

'Here.' Robert handed Absolom his wallet, containing the wages for the bar staff. 'Go. Get out of here as fast as you can.' Absolom reached, took the money. He kissed his mother's tear-washed cheeks. For a long moment they stared at each other and silent words filled the gap between them. Then he left, closing the door quietly behind him.

Mary stood there, afraid to move. Robert stood there, unable to move.

For this was the last coherent act of Robert's life. In that room, his battered brain gave up the struggle and didn't bother with anything again.

Near the end of my high school career I began to get it right. I learned the importance of Acting; being able to instantly translate my entire personality into a cardboard cutout, exactly appropriate to whatever my audience or surroundings required.

When the paper-bagged bottle of brandy was passed around I learned to take a token swig. When the boys indulged in ludicrous fictions about their knee-trembling experiences with girls, I learnt to develop a knowing air.

I joined Societies. I did First Aid (to avoid having to participate in the ludicrous antics of the Cadet Corps) and managed to avoid sports by lying about my health.

At home, things were bitter and twisted. I forgot to mention that without permission and without consultation, Mother and Father had bred again, in 1952. They produced another son so soon after I had made my entrance into what I had thought would be a grateful world.

The other son was called Barry. I didn't like him from the first. Mainly because I knew that he was a reincarnation of Bratislaw Plowsky, a minor Polish poet of the mid-nineteenth century.

I had never met Plowsky, but I knew his mother. In another incarnation, of course.

Inevitably, I refused to call him anything other than Plowsky, which caused him some anger.

Shortly after we met the first signs of hatred appeared. We had different ideas about the amount of air which should be allowed into the bedroom at night. We locked wills about whether the door should be open or closed. We clashed over waking up times on weekends. And so, when we became able to articulate our mutual dislike, Plowsky and I began to express our feelings in violent ways. Some were subtle, some were not. Like flying bricks (not subtle) to turds in bed (deliciously subtle), dead snakes in the pockets of school jackets. (Subtle. Had the snake been alive, it would not have been subtle.)

And, of course, unsubtle screaming, tearing rows.

After a few years of this the parents, undeterred by their failure to produce a harmonious household so far bred again. This time they managed a girl.

She was quite perfect. China-dollish, simpering, sweet as toffee-apple and just as sticky. So the parents called her Michelle.

Plowsky and I soon fixed all that.

We were vicious rivals, remember, locked in a battle to the death. But when a threat invaded the closed boundaries of our little Kingdom of Hate we joined together to eliminate it.

The parents actually assisted us – me and Plowsky – to become allies. With characteristic stable-door diplomacy they brought in some builders and added three bedrooms to the house. For the first time in my life I could have the window open and the door closed at night. I could jerk off in front of my very own full-length mirror while Plowsky jerked off in front of his next door.

So, as two independent, self-sufficient, territorially secure nations, Plowsky and I became allies in the thrilling project of reducing Mummy's little toffee-apple to a quivering mess of tears. Whenever possible.

Like furious seas we battered the cliffs of her self-confidence. And when we had reduced them to soggy rubble, we just kept going.

How do I feel now about all that? I feel as if I've stamped on a butterfly. Helped to crush at least one gorgeous wing.

Meanwhile Daniel was becoming very rich. Teeth set, eyes flaring, stomach tied in knots, he was ploughing through all opposition to make his company the biggest manufacturer of built-in-obsolescence kitchens. With unusual foresight, he jumped aboard a DC3 in 1956 and travelled to America. There, in between bouts of machinery, material and pattern buying, he managed to have at least two brushes with infidelity and three brushes with the law. He returned laden with guilt, gifts and, most importantly, the means with which to make plastic-covered kitchens, the design revolution of the late 'fifties.

I was happy when he went away and miserable when he came back. Daniel and I just didn't like each other. He wanted me to be a great cricketer. I wanted to be a snug slug in a book-lined room left alone to read and jerk off and sleep.

Besides, Daniel didn't have time for his family. It is a sad truth that if you want to be very rich, and wipe out the memories of a poor childhood, and prove that your stepmother-in-law is wrong, the family has to come fourth.

This didn't please Anne who loved Daniel. When he spent so much time away she became miserable, lost, bitter. And when he did come back, coping with the constant tension and his outbursts of anger wasn't her idea of marriage.

It was always the same after one of his trips: first there would be the tearful lovers' meeting at the airport, then the tearing row in the bedroom. Followed by the inevitable reconciliation which would involve love-making with wild groans of forced delight, which would filter underneath my bedroom door like taunts.

Anne decided to get re-involved in politics.

In Britain the bored wife of a nouveau-riche businessman joins the Women's Institute, or the CND. Or goes to evening classes in Late Renaissance Art or French for Beginners. But this was South Africa. Mother ended up in the Black Sash.

The Black Sash: staunch barrel-legged dames of Conscience with stone-carved faces in Socialist-Realist style, sashes of mourning draped about gargantuan shoulders, standing on traffic islands holding their protest banners under the noses of an uneasy police force who didn't quite know how to handle these obviously mad women, daughters of, wives of some of the most influential businessmen in the country. Valkyries, Fates, Norns, Heroines.

Laughed at, jeered at by passing White Trash. Targets for rotten eggs, tomatoes and worse, they served two important purposes: first, they gave the white trash a visible outlet for their hatred of anything which threatened their security; second, they salved their own consciences and those of their husbands. They were doing something. While Daddy paid his black workers nuppence a week, while servants slaved away in the kitchen and garden, Mummy was Doing Something.

So Anne would come home from a protest spattered with egg, tomato and even shit. We children would cluster around her numbly. She would be weeping with frustration. We would cluck and feel terribly proud. To us, she was defying the entire Government, Police and Army of the country. Later, Father would come home. She would weep again. They would go off to the bedroom and fight. Then, those groans and cries.

The Government wasn't interested in those women. Then. They considered them harmless.

One

Many people get so tangled up in the lives they happen to be living, they quite forget all those common knowledge things one instantly remembers after a death.

Like, we've had four atomic wars on earth already, hence the Ice Ages, so what's all the fuss about? That kinda stuff.

You know that feeling, just after death when you've dumped the body and done all the passageway and light bit? I always say, 'Oh boy, here we are again!' With a sigh. Can you remember that feeling? Like waking up in the morning after a dream-filled night.

One of my deaths stays in my mind. I imagine it will through many more lives too. Me: Sixteen years old, Polish, flying a biplane 1916, over a battlefield, shot down, never saw my assailant, crunch, fire all around, struggle out of plane, stagger a few yards, look back, there's my body still in the plane, burning. Deep sigh. Oh boy, here we go again.

Another: Me an ancient minister to some petty Middle Eastern potentate in the fourteenth century. One night his brother and assassins burst into palace.

Kill guards, storm into bedroom containing the Caliph and his wife. I stand in their way and say, very reasonably, most earnestly, 'You don't *have* to do this, you know,' but they stab me anyway and go on, I suppose, to kill my master and mistress. What I can't remember is *why* they didn't have to kill the K & Q. Was the Caliph going to abdicate? Did he have a terminal illness? Why didn't he *tell* his idiot brother in time to save my life? Oh boy, here we go again. Actually, that time, I hung about and haunted people for a while. I was, after all, a bit annoyed.

That death is the root of my love for bitter endings, cliffhangers, black comedy.

Real life is the best joke of all. That's why this book is all true.

Pieter grew up like a train, a pair of wheelsets on different parallel tracks leading in the same direction.

His schoolfellows, his parents, all his white friends and relatives carried these misapprehensions on their broad Boere backs: Blacks are:

1. DIRTY
2. STUPID
3. LAZY
4. DESTINED THEREFORE TO BE SERVILE FOREVER.

They justified their prejudice by referring to the Bible, the story of Cain and Abel. The belief being: Whites are the children of Abel (the Goodie), and the Blacks the children of Cain (the Baddie). And hath not the Lord said the children of Cain shall be ' . . . hewers of wood and drawers of water'?

Afrikaners hadn't made the obvious logical leap which would have demonstrated that: Some Blacks were dirty because the Whites had all the showers and baths and Christian Dior perfume.

Some Blacks seemed stupid because the Government

68

spent R2 per year per child on their education, while spending R200 per year per white child. (1966.)

Besides, many South African Blacks discovered that there were many advantages in appearing stupid to the White Boss.

Of *course* many Blacks were lazy. Wouldn't *you* be if you had employers like that?

So prejudice feeds on itself.

'Prejudice'. The word means exactly that; to pre-judge. The mechanism is interesting. It is rather like a filter formed in early life which filters *out* any contradictory information. It is self-perpetuating and no amount of logic will shift it.

The other rail Piet's feet were on was built and laid by Umfaan.

Umfaan, ancient anomaly constructed of dust. When he yawned you could see shadows of maggots writhing amongst his tonsils. No one knew where he came from or how old he was. He didn't know himself. But when he spoke he was vibrant and full of humour. And young as I am.

I don't know where he came from either, which is strange, as I invented him.

I can speculate from clues in his stories, though this is probably futile, as he is the World's Greatest Liar.

Here is one of the stories he told Piet Mostert who sat on the dusty ground under a thorn tree listening adoringly to the perfect voice of an old man sitting on a log:

Justice and the Orange Tree

'There are in this world, little piccaninny, Thirty-Six Just Men. Yes, only thirty-six.

'The Thirty-Six do not know they are the Just Men, the Chosen of God. All they know is, they can see with

69

a clear and perfect vision into the hearts of men. They can sort out *any* dispute because they can tell who is right.

'Now one day a Farmer came in from the fields and found his wife lying naked on the bed, crying.

' "*O maar Jesus*, Marie, what are you doing at this time of the day naked on the bed?"

'His wife could only weep some more, so he asked a second time, "*Nou maar*, Marie, what is all this weeping and ungodly nakedness at this time of day?"

'Finally, he managed to get some sense out of the woman. "O Jakob," she cried. "I was lying here reading my book, about to make the supper when in came Umjona, the Garden Boy!"

' "Now what was the Garden Boy doing in this house?"

' "Nevermind. He threw me on the bed and he – had his way with me!" '

Piet interrupted with the Obvious Question and was given a quick sex lecture, too intimate and graphic to go into here; but suffice it to say the scales fell from Piet's eyes, he added two and two together and got, unsurprisingly, four.

Lucky when you think about it. Neither Hester nor Japie could possibly have given Piet a useful sex education as they considered masturbation sinful and sex outside marriage as something to be done when God wasn't looking.

I never had any sex education from my parents either. I quite envy Piet. I was entirely self-taught, my early ideas gained from lies and hints. At sixteen I still thought sperm was transferred from man to woman while dancing. Which was why parents always touched when they danced and we kids had to do no-touch dances like the Twist.

Piet was better informed at a younger age. This could explain a lot of things.

' "So couldn't you fight him off?" asked the angry Farmer.

' "*Ag, mos,* he's so *strong,*" she said, going all quivery.

'So the Farmer runs and gets his shotgun and goes chasing the Garden Boy.

'He goes to the kaffirhuts, no Garden Boy.

'He searches the garden, no Garden Boy.

'He goes to the orchard and there, high in the branches of an orange tree, sits the Garden Boy.

' "Hey *jou!*" shouted the Farmer, waving his shotgun. "Come down!"

' "No, my baas, if I come down you will shoot me dead."

' "Come down right now," the Farmer ordered. "I won't shoot you. I only want to talk."

'But Umjona was not stupid. "No, my baas, I don't believe you. I am going to stay here until I die from old age."

' "What will you live on, you stupid kaffir?"

' "Oranges, my baas, oranges," said the cheeky fellow, making sure that there were a good many branches between his angry Boss's shotgun and himself.

' "In that case I will stay here until you die."

' "And what will *you* live on, baas?"

' "I will live on roast chicken, beans, potatoes, carrots and *soetkoek,*" and he shouted to his wife to send him out some dinner.

'For five days the Farmer sat there under the tree and the Garden Boy sat above him being careful not to hit the Baas with orange peel or the products of his bowels or bladder.'

Piet interrupted with another obvious question. Two words answered him.

'The story became the talk of the town. The Dominee came and tried to reason with them. The Police Captain came and offered to call the Fire Service to get the Kaffir down. But the Farmer said it was *his* problem and he would deal with it in his way. The people from the newspaper interviewed everybody but ran off when the Farmer pointed his shotgun at them.

'One day the Town Drunk came wandering by. His name was Umfaan, but he was not me.

' "Ai baasie!" he cried. "Have you got a squirrel in that tree?"

'The Farmer wiped his lips with his sleeve, dropping bits of koeksuster on to his lap. "No, you stupid man, this creature has interfered with my wife."

' "And what are you going to do with him when he finally falls down like a ripe orange at your feet?"

' "I am going to remove his black hide and make a sjambok out of it."

' "What a great crime he must have done, baas!"

' "Now go away, *moomish*," said the Farmer, "and leave me to my misery."

' "Can I talk to this villain first, baas?" the Drunk asked.

' "Go on, boy, talk to him and go away."

' "Hey Umjona! Unjani!" the Drunk greeted the hollow-eyed Garden Boy. "This Farmer wants to kill you."

' "I know that, Umfaan! He thinks I seduced his missus."

' "And *did* you do this thing, Umjona?" asked Umfaan.

' "What, *that* cow?" said the Boy. "I couldn't make it with *that* fat ugly old hag if she paid me."

' "WHAT!" howled the Farmer.

' "What happened on that day, Umjona?"

' "It was like this, Umfaan. She asks me to go to her room with some cut flowers. Then she offers me £1 if I will get it out."

' "WHAT!" howled the Farmer again like a lion with his balls in a twist.

' "My John Thomas, baas," said the Garden Boy, not understanding. "So I said no. Then she offers me £5 to

72

get my trousers off. Then I refuse so she throws her clothes off and tries to grab me. But I run away, Umjona, wouldn't you? Then the Baas comes home."

' "You *didn't* rape her?" the astonished Farmer asked. "Why?"

' "I told you, she is ugly, very ugly, my baas. I am very sorry."

'And suddenly the Farmer realised it was true what the Garden Boy said because his wife was indeed very ugly and the Farmer himself hadn't made it with her for twelve years.

' "Why didn't you tell me before?" asked the Farmer.

' "You didn't *ask* me, my baas."

' "So there you are, my baas," said the Drunk. "A happy ending." And he lurched off into the sunset while the Garden Boy climbed off the tree.

' "Happy for *you*," said the Farmer and discharged one barrel of the shotgun into Umfaan's retreating back.

' "Why did you do that?" the terrified Garden Boy asked.

' "Because I am *never* wrong," said the Farmer, shooting Umjona with the other barrel. "And furthermore, I don't want any witnesses!" '

Piet laughed and laughed until Umfaan stared him in the eye and said, 'There was nothing funny about that story.'

'But why, Umfaan? I thought it was a joke story.'

'It's not a joke. The Farmer shot a Just Man, and God had to find another one.'

'Which one was the Just Man?'

The old fellow shook his head, laughing, clapped Piet playfully across an ear. 'Umfaan, of course! If Umjona was a Just Man, he wouldn't have climbed down from the tree.'

Two

'VOTE NO'. The graffiti everywhere. No to the suffering of the people. No to detentions without trial. No to the erosion of democracy. But mostly NO to the declaration of the Republic of South Africa.

Membership of the British Commonwealth was considered by the oppressed and their white liberal allies as the only hopeful factor in the South African tragedy. It meant that somewhere, 'oversea', there was a body led by Her Majesty the Queen of the Vanishing Empire, which would, godlike, reach down and save the suffering millions in the remote southern tip of the African continent.

A Deus Ex Machina.

By Act of Parliament, South Africa left the Commonwealth on May 31st, 1961, after a token referendum in which only Whites voted.

Despair in the townships. And anger. Protests, strikes, innumerable meetings in which the anger and despair were turned into millions of bitter resolutions: to oppose, oppose and oppose. So the military was mobilised. Ten thousand people were arrested under the Twelve Day Law, by which detention without trial became part of the South African way of life.

And the Black Nationalist Movements realised that violent opposition was the only way to change this satanic status quo.

Absolom Molapo travelled around the country addressing meetings: in halls, on stony football fields, in crowded living-rooms. Always ready to run if the police should pour in through the windows.

Which they did, three times.

The South African Police is a terrifying animal, composed of some of the stupidest and most vicious men in the world. It is a blind, deaf and dumb beast, armour-plated, covered all over with bristling, poisonous spines.

A police sergeant confronting my mother, picked up for obstruction. 'I don't understand you people. Are you all *mad*? You Communists want to rule the world and what will happen to all of us, hey?'

'I'm not a Communist—'

'Don't lie to me. If you support another race against your own you are a traitor. You *must* be a Communist.'

Daddy bailed her out, of course. Fined Twenty Rand. Nice white woman like that, what a shame.

They weren't so lenient with Blacks or Coloureds. They had all these clever little games, like electrodes to attach to sensitive bits of the body; like refusing toilet facilities for three days; like attacks on the genitals. A boring catalogue of brutality: there is no limit to human invention when it comes to inflicting pain on others.

They do all this and yet still believe, deep in their hearts, that they are right and God is on their side; that they are fighting for the very survival of the white race and biblical values and true morality. This struggle justifies everything.

Black and White. Cain and Abel. Good and Evil.

Mary Molapo lived in a place on street fourteen, Soweto. That was not the name of the street. No one knew the name of the street. It was just the fourteenth street when you turned left from the station. All the streets looked alike. When you walked home from the station, you had to count them off. And if you were drunk at the time – as you probably would be if you had been visiting Mary Molapo – you had to keep your wits about you to find your way to your bed. And if it happened to be night, you were risking death, because only 40 per cent of Soweto had electricity and the township was more crime-ridden than Harlem.

So you made sure that any party you went to was an all-night party.

Don't imagine that the townships were places of

misery and suffering only. Suffering breeds religion. The religions were two: the worship of Christ, in many guises, and the worship of alcohol. Many worshipped both.

So townships and 'Locations' were seething loud laughing drunken crying places of parties and crime and prayer, where when people laugh, they laugh loudly, and when they cry they do so with wracking deep eternal sorrow, and God and His Angels cry too.

Gangs ruled the streets, knives flashed like teeth, blood escaped and sank into the ground every day, every night. So common as to be cheap, police can't be blamed for giving up.

Women ruled the homes, hearts, families. The Amanyano: huge Christ-obsessed ladies who sang like angels, whose wrenching magnificent harmonies Handel would have loved. Ham-sized hands to keep their men controlled. The Methodist Mothers, with their red blouses, black skirts and white hats. The Zionists who, like a Lost Tribe of Israel, sported Stars of David and dressed in blue and white. Starched, blindingly clean and crisply ironed.

Begging God to come down and *DO* Something.

Above them all sat the Township Superintendent, the White Boss who could point a quivering finger at some sinner who didn't have quite the right papers and roar like an Old Testament Prophet, 'Thou art Endorsed Out!' Which meant the miscreant had to go forthwith to his or her 'Homeland', which he or she had probably never seen. Off to Kwa Zulu with you. Take thyself to the Transkei. Thou art banished for offending against the Great God Apartheid.

Like Canute and the waves, community leaders tried to hold back the waves of crime, of drink, of sorrow. The Priests, the Mayor, the Police.

The people weren't all poor. There were the Black Fat Cats who lived off the people, growing fatter still from drink, drugs, sex.

The most popular drug was marijuana, called 'dagga', skyf or grass. Marijuana, which South Africa's climate makes exceptionally well. It is an integral part of black life, and of the Indians' and Coloureds' as well. But unlike her sisters in Pondoland, with their ground-brushing skirts and proud bared breasts and their long wooden pipes filled with the mindbendingest grass you've ever smoked, Mary Molapo had never smoked grass for she was after all very religious. Though the smell of it – like old socks and ammonia – was as familiar to her as Chanel perfume is to the white chairlady of the Johannesburg Bridge Club. This despite the fact that she had sold the stuff to many visitors to the little room on the top floor of Killarney Heights.

We find her in Soweto. The Stones had finally 'retired' her in her sixty-eighth year. Her hands were knobbly, arthritic sculptures with only vestigial movement. Her spine was almost calcified rigid. Her life had become a movie seen through a fog of pain. She was in love with Death, and prayed for him to come and get her.

She suspected, though she didn't admit it, that her pain was a punishment for her schizophrenic life-style: the Manyano on the one hand, and the shebeen on the other. She wasn't too worried. She was sure she could square things with God, once she confronted Him face to face.

Hazel had decided to retire her after the Man in the Room incident. Technically, she could have thrown her into the street with nothing but she swallowed her indignation, borrowed £200 from Daniel and gave it to Mary to 'buy half of her sister's house'. Hazel had not forgotten Mary's heroism at the time of the Accident and though she would never admit to it, there was a softness in her heart for the black woman.

But once out of sight, she was entirely forgotten by the whole Stone family. Especially Robert, who couldn't even remember his own name.

The 'house' wasn't a house, as such. It was a shebeen. It was shared with Mary's younger sister Lillian.

Auntie Lillian was a blowsy, laughter-made woman who ran a shebeen known as the Red House, because on its opening night the greatest gang-leader of the time had bloodied the doormat with a famous murder.

Lillian was delighted with the events that led to her sister's joining her, and especially with the £100 which Mary had – reluctantly – given her (keeping the other hundred to herself, of course).

Lillian and Mary had planned for a long time to run the biggest, most professional, most popular shebeen in Soweto and they needed the money for bribes and bigger premises.

Did I give you the impression that Mary was a shrinking violet, even a saint? Wrong. Don't forget she had run a backyard shebeen for years (supplied with drink by her resourceful younger sister). She had saved £400 of her own in all those years.

Her ambition was to leave a great sum of money behind her when she died. Why?

I don't know.

So she became a full partner in the new Red House shebeen and sat all day and all night in a corner, or so it seemed, pouring vast quantities of good KWV brandy down her throat, trying to kill either the pain or herself, whichever came first. Joking with the men. Buying drinks for the women. Emitting little blasts of laughter.

But this night the shebeen was quiet, though full. Grim men in hats and suits stood by the doors. The house was packed with anxious men and women. There was a feeling that something fantastically important was about to happen.

Absolom Molapo entered, greeting the sentry at the door who responded reverently. Absolom was in his thirties, but looked older. He was crag-faced, grim and had the air of authority of an old cardinal, though he wore a suit which looked as if it had last been worn in a

78

gangster movie. His shirt cuffs were black and frayed. Sweat darkened the armpits. The room was chokingly hot and smelled of beer, tobacco, sweat and fear.

Mary sat in her corner and stared at this stranger whom she loved so much. That he had so much power! She was proud. She prayed that men like this would lead the new South Africa. Men she knew.

Everyone rose to their feet and started clapping restrainedly, trying to keep the sound down, praying that there were no passing policemen.

'Mayibuye!' they cried, but softly. 'Mayibuye; Afrika!'

'Thank you, thank you my friends. Thank you all for coming.' Absolom motioned for the noise to stop. 'And thank you, my mother and my dear auntie, for giving us this place tonight for this meeting in this dangerous time.

> I am honoured that you have given me this chance to tell you about the struggle, and where we have reached in the battle for our rights.
>
> Our white oppressors are growing stronger every day. They have betrayed the people of South Africa by pulling us out of the Commonwealth without the consent of our people.
>
> That is not the most terrible blow. What has the Commonwealth done for us? Did they stop the Government making even our women carry passes in 1959? Did they stop the Sharpeville massacre? Did they stop the suffering of the people, day, after day, after day?

Little Muna shifted in his seat. He was a police informer. He was memorising every word. He was known as Weasel to his acquaintances in the township.

And to his friends in the police.

> Did they stop this State of Emergency, which
> makes even this meeting illegal and threatens
> each one of us to detention without trial?
> No, my friends. Our people are in peril.
> Our leaders are all in danger. Mandela is
> running. Sisulu is running. I am running.
> No, when the People are in peril, only the
> People can save itself.

Muna waited for the call to Revolution. This would be
the final evidence which would get Molapo's neck
stretched for treason.

> What can we do now? What? I ask you my
> friends. We have tried negotiations. We have
> tried protests, strikes.
> I will tell you, there is only one course left. I
> say it with sadness, my friends, because I am
> a man of peace.
> But what is called for is a weapon. The
> weapon we have forged is a spear. It is the
> Spear of the Nation. It is called Umkonto!
> Umkonto We Sizwe. The Spear of the Nation.
> Umkonto We Sizwe is the creation of the
> ANC, the PAC and all our comrades who
> desire freedom.
> My brothers and sisters, it is time for us to
> join together. We need friends, we need
> members, and we need money.
> Harness your anger! Let the people stand
> together! Let us all give our all to the Nation.
> The Black Nation, which is Zulu, Sotho,
> Xhosa, Ndebele, Venda, Shangaan, Coloured,
> Indian and many I have not mentioned, in-
> cluding even those Whites who support us.
> In 1950 the Whites made us separate and

inferior, with their population registration. That was twelve years ago, and we didn't rise. They made a joke of us in 1959, with their so-called Self-Government Act, by which they tried to steal our lands and banish us to so-called Homelands, the driest, poorest thirteen per cent of the country. And we didn't rise. Now they make us all live in fear with their State of Emergency.

Now I want you all to rise up. Rise up! And sing with me, for all our brothers and sisters in detention, for the future of South Africa.

They stood, like a church congregation, even Mary stood though her joints cried for the world, and they sang, 'Nkosi Sikelele Afrika'. And the doors burst in and men with brown uniforms poured in with knobkerries and sjamboks and guns drawn. People screamed and writhed away from these flashing sources of pain. There was no escape. Absolom knew that this time he couldn't get away. He stood with great dignity waiting for the tidal wave to reach him, searching the smoky gloom for his mother's face.

By the time they reached him and closed the handcuffs about his numbly extended wrists his mother was already dead. A brief explosion of pain had finished her pain and released her.

Here we go again.

Three

I was twelve when I became an activist. Silly little pimpled know-it-all adolescent, putting up VOTE NO posters, despite Mother's apprehension and Father's ignorance. Sneaking out of the house at midnight with

81

an armload of posters and a pot of wallpaper-paste. Tiptoeing into the dead-quiet streets with my load of guilt.

Plowsky came with me once or twice. No one else came at all. I learnt my first lesson: Friendship is not a blank cheque.

Somewhere about this time, Mother betrayed me and I didn't forgive her for many years.

She was very worried for my safety, I suppose, on reflection. So she told Daniel.

There was a row of mythic proportions: Father a thundering rhino in a piano shop.

I ran out of the house.

Father pursued me in the car.

I ran along the pavement, the 1957 Chevrolet hurtling after me, Daniel totally out of control at the wheel, trying to run the car at me and avoid the trees on the sidewalk.

I jumped over a garden wall and ran to a friend's house, where I hid terrified in his bedroom, and wouldn't speak.

By the time his parents had phoned my parents, Daniel was drunk, calm, and ashamed.

I am ashamed when I think about this incident. Had I known then how Daniel was fighting, in his way, for what I regarded as *my* beliefs, I would have kept very quiet and stayed at home.

A Barmitzvah

How do you make a precocious mixed-up teenager with nothing but bitterness for his parents, with nothing but misery at school, learn a bunch of mindless words in a foreign language? And sing them to a rambling, antique tune?

You bribe him.

It has worked for thousands of years. In ancient Palestine, in the shtetls in Russia, in ghettos all over the world. 'Mummy, why must I learn all this?' 'Think of the *presents*, my son, think of the presents.'

I thought of the presents. Fountain pens by the dozen (the equivalent of the wedding toast-racks). Sets of encyclopaedias. Great big books about Israel. Subscriptions to the *National Geographic*. Silver-plated platters engraved 'To Darling . . . on the Occasion of his Barmitzvah'. The silver Kaddish goblets.

Nope. Nothing there of any interest.

But what about the *money*, my son?

Now that pounds had become rands, money always sounded like more than it was. The exchange rate being two rands to the pound.

I figured on about three hundred rands, based on the loot contemporaries had earned. Not bad for a couple of hours' torture.

So like a good boy I trotted off to Barmitzvah lessons twice a week, my yarmulka and prayerbook hidden in my jacket.

My companion, a black collie called Mac, a reincarnation of Zhakski, the Russian clown 1906 – 1944, insisted on accompanying me on the fifteen-minute walk to the Rabbi's house. The walk was mostly along the banks of a little stream I called The River, which carried a variety of noxious liquids from the sewerage farm a few miles upstream.

Mac's reason for accompanying me was that, once I was safely head-down in the Rabbi's dining-room, he could practise cartwheels and headstands unobserved, as no one else ever walked by the river due to the quite incredible smell that accompanied its picturesque meanderings. Mac was determined to be reborn as a clown again, because he hadn't quite got the hang of it last time when he was so forcibly removed from earth by a German tank. I suspect that I may in fact have been driving that tank; I seem to remember rather too much German, and the timing would be about right. I just can't remember the last life as vividly as some of the others.

I remember, for example, that this is not my first life in Africa. Though the death is more memorable than the life. I was ten. A noise in the bedroom one night. I woke. A burglar. A shot. The extraordinary sensation of a bullet tearing into my chest like a blow, finding the heart and everything shutting down, then Oh boy, etc.

So Mac did his cartwheels, headstands, card tricks and so on while I chanted '*Adonai Elohaynu . . .*' and so on.

When the ancient Jews decided to make the ceremony of manhood happen to boys of thirteen (only *boys*, note – the Batmitzvah is a recent invention), they were either not thinking or being diabolically sadistic.

Was I a boy soprano or a young baritone? Unfortunately my larynx couldn't make up its mind and often changed in mid-phrase.

This is a problem suffered by many Jewish boys, undergoing the Jewish equivalent of the custom some black tribes have of sending young boys into the bush for seven days without so much as a spear between them.

So when the absurd day dawned, my throat didn't know what the hell it was going to do, and neither did I.

On the lawn a marquee.

The house bristles with starched servants rushing about with trays, relatives known and unknown looking for someone to give their fountain pens to, parents looking for me, me looking for Mac, panic and more panic.

Granny Zelda, who had confounded everybody by not following Mossie to the grave thirteen years ago – she had decided on brain-death instead – sits on a deckchair in the garden muttering, 'They're trying to poison me, you know,' to any caterer or relative who will listen.

Father struts about the house pretending to be in charge. Actually he's looking for Hymie Feinsteen who's due any minute and with whom Father wants to discuss A Very Big Deal.

Mother keeps rushing into her room to have hysterics then rushing out again to make sure the canapés are OK.

Robert, Hazel and Anthony sit on a bench in the garden doing a Gainsborough imitation. With the difference that the squire doesn't carry a gun which is lucky considering his head is as empty as the wind. The son is hoping, without conviction, that there may be young male guests of the willing kind. The wife is wishing she were at home and wondering what their part is in this barbaric ceremony and would Robert do anything disgraceful.

It had taken her two hours to get him out of bed but she had brought him despite Anthony's protests to show Anne that her father was still alive, though emptied out like a slop bucket.

But now it's time to make the Grand Procession to the Synagogue and this creates a Problem.

The Synagogue is next door to the Rabbi's house. Since it's the Sabbath, and I'm being barmitzvah'd today, the Rabbi would naturally expect my family to walk to Shul. The Short Cut means the odorous walk by the river. The long way is pretty long and there's no way Robert or Zelda would manage it.

Mother had yanked Daniel away from his desperate discussion with Hymie Feinsteen and insisted that he solve the problem. 'Right,' says Daniel. 'It's simple. We'll take three cars, park around the corner, bingo! What the Rev doesn't know won't hurt him. Come along everybody.'

'No,' I say. 'If you want me to be Jewish today I can't possibly ride in a car.'

'Are you mad?' Zelda shrieks, emerging briefly from her paranoid world. 'On Shabbat! You want me to go in a car?'

'You *came here* in a car this morning, Mama,' says Daniel. 'Now don't *fuss*—'

'Nonsense, vot are you trying to do to me?' She turns to Hazel who nods sympathetically. 'They are trying to kill me, you know,' she explains.

'Look Granny, it's quite simple, you and me can walk by the river. We'll meet them there.' I am getting anxious. We have half an hour to get there.

'Me? *Valk*? I am an old lady, I can't valk.'

'Do you *want* to see your grandchild barmitzvah'd?' Daniel is exasperated and will be very angry soon.

'Don't you *dare* talk to me like that. You see?' Hazel nods. 'If he can't poison me he vants me to have heart attack. Come, ve go.' She grabs me by an arm. 'Do you have your tallis? Yarmulka? Hev you got your book? Come! If I die on the vay, you leave me there.'

She propels me out of the front gate, down to the bottom of the road. There, we have to climb over a fence to get to the river, which Granny manages with incredible agility. She has turned girlish and shrieky with delight.

Granny Zelda was a tiny little thing, made almost entirely of bone. What skin there was clung to the bones in puffy white runnels. She had a fascinating moustache which made me and Plowsky speculate endlessly about her sexual orientation.

'I vos a terrible tomboy ven I vas young,' she explains with a wink. We make our way down the track to the river and suddenly there is a vooshing sound in the long grass and Granny screams, 'Argh! It's lions! This is a plot!'

'Don't be silly, it's only Mac,' who comes grinning out of the grass saying, Oh good, are we going to our Barmy lesson then?

'It's all *right*, Granny, he's a friend,' I reassure her.

'Tenks God!' Mac goes up to her and says Hi. She starts, looks at him very carefully, 'Is this yours? Vot's his name?'

'Mac, Granny, you've met him many times before.'

'That's vhy. I knew I knew him from somevere.' Mac is staring at her, ears cocked, quite as intently as she had stared at him.

'Look Mac, I have to explain something to you. Today's the day,' I say. What day? 'The day of the Actual Barmy. What I've been studying for all this time.' So you want me to come with you to hold your hand? 'Don't be silly. I want you to stay well away.' What kind of friend am I to stay well away when my friend needs me? 'Look Mac, they don't let dogs in Shul.' A dog! A *dog* am I? First you say I'm your friend now you call me a dog. Hah! 'Please Mac, be reasonable.' Reasonable! HAH!

Granny is watching this exchange with full comprehension. She's one of the only humans I've met who can understand dog language. Probably because she's crazy as a loon.

'You!' She points a bone at him, 'I *know* you!' What? 'I *know* you. Maybe you don't remember me. Smolensk, hah? 1916?'

OK, Granny, I think, not comprehending, this is it. Over the top. Flipped for ever. Looped the loop. White coats time.

The dog sets up a howl and howls and howls. Granny drapes some of her bones around him and hugs him, comforting, if angular. 'You go,' she says. 'I'll catch you up later. Ve have a lot of private things to discuss. Now go!'

I'm not too happy about this, oh no. How does one explain a missing granny? I can't say she is sitting on a river bank reminiscing with a dog.

She throws a stone at me. 'Go! Can't you see this is private?' Fearful for the integrity of my skull, soaked in misgivings, I leave.

I arrive at the Synagogue to find Plowsky waiting outside. 'Where the hell have you been? You're fifteen minutes late! They've held up the service for you. Where's Granny?'

'I can't explain. She'll be here. Come on.'

We go in. Sit in the family pew, wait for the call. 'Where's your grandmother?' Father hisses.

'She's coming, Father.'

'Oh my God.' He looks like a prophet who had just heard that the world will end at twelve o'clock. 'Have you left her alone?'

'Well, yes, or no. No.'

'If you've left her alone I'll kill you. Barmitzvah or no Barmitzvah.'

Groan. Just then, the *chazan* calls me to the *bimah* to read my allocated extract from the Scroll.

Which starts OK in boy soprano. But *that* doesn't last. BLETHERblether blether blether! CRACK! Bletherbletherblether a-men! Blether blether blether (this sounds OK if only I can keep it up)! CRACK! Oh shit blether blether blether a disturbance at the door blether bletherblether oooops! CRACK! Bleth— stop dead because Mac has just entered. Some wag has draped a tallis about his shoulders and placed a yarmulka on his head. He walks in, up the aisle to the *bimah*. So this is the famous Shul, is it? What happens now?

'Mac! Go and sit down! I told you not to come.' Me, leaning over the *bimah*, gesticulating wildly. All right, don't *panic*. Plowsky is yelling 'Mac! Get out!' Daniel is holding his head in his hands and pretending he's a thousand miles away.

There is a stir in the women's gallery above us as Granny pushes her way into a row of seats, looking for Hazel – who she has decided is a Kindred Spirit. She sees everyone looking up and waves gaily, like a little girl.

'Somebody' – the Rabbi has assumed command – 'get that dog out!' Grim-faced men surround Mac, who pleads, What have I done?

'Vot!' Granny shrieks from above like a demented angel. 'How DARE you throw a Jew out of a Synagogue! I *know* you, Newman! You vant to poison me as well! Vell, you can't—' Mother pushes her way through the astounded ladies and tries to put a restraining arm about the siren's shoulders. 'Get off! How DARE you treat Jews like this! Nazis! Nazis!' she screams.

All thoughts of continuing the service are evaporating as the chaos mounts. The women have assumed the characters of hens amongst whom a fox has been dropped. The men are trying to surround the bemused dog who has decided that this is an ideal opportunity to display his headstands and cartwheels.

'This is the House of God, for godsake!' howls the Rabbi, seeing his life's work collapsing into chaos.

Granny has made her way to the rail on the gallery. 'If you lay a hand on that innocent dog I will jump! I will!' She teeters on the rail.

'Oh Jesus – oops! Don't jump! I beg you, lady, don't jump!' the Rabbi cries, rushing for the exit, with the intention of mounting the stairs to the gallery.

That'll show them, says Mac, you jump, darling. I'll join you soon. We've got business to finish.

'Don't jump, Granny, for godsake!' I yell.

'Get DOWN, Mama!' Daniel commands.

Just then the Rabbi bursts into the gallery, trips over a seat, falls onto Mrs Levine who collapses against Mrs Cohen whose bag strikes little Michelle in the face whose hands fly up and knock Mother against Granny who sails out above the congregation with an 'Oyyyyyyy Vay!' and falls with a scarcely audible thunk.

On top of Hymie Feinsteen.

Hah! You thought I was heading toward another 'here we go again' situation. No. You see, Hymie is a huge balloon of a man, a lovely soft mountain of flesh to fall onto, and Granny was scarcely hurt, despite being mercifully knocked unconscious by an elbow.

Mac dashed outside to find a car to die under. Here we go again.

And after the Ambulance and all that had removed Granny, the Rabbi insisted on continuing the service.

I was devastated at the loss of my friend, embarrassed as only a teenager can be by the behaviour of my granny, and I sang the remainder of my portion exceedingly badly.

The delayed luncheon in the marquee was more like a wake.

Of course the preceding narrative is all nonsense, though things could well have happened that way.

Granny *did* have a fling with a young clown in 1916, just before leaving Russia. Had she realised that Mac was that same clown, she would certainly have acted in the way described.

I *did* have severe problems with a breaking voice during my Barmitzvah ceremony. It was bloody embarrassing, and ensured that, from the age of thirteen, I never willingly entered a synagogue again.

Neither, incidentally, did Anthony. As we were leaving the synagogue, suffering the muted congratulations of the congregation, a young man came up to Anthony and slapped him soundly across the face. 'Don't you DARE stare at me like that!' he said, and vanished into the crowd.

Anthony decided that he didn't like Jews. And so did I.

Oh, and Mac *did* die under a car.

Four

My teenage years began with Sharpeville and the death of John F. Kennedy.

Most people who were old enough to read when JFK was shot remember that day exceedingly well. I do. Sunday morning, I fetched the papers from the garden gate, saw the four-inch headline, KENNEDY DEAD, woke Anne and Daniel; we all felt as if an era had ended and Things Could Only Get Worse.

They did. I've told you about school, that was pretty worse.

Other things were not so bad. I began collecting antiques and classical music. I discovered opera. Daniel had a boxed set of *Tosca*, which contained a libretto. I read the libretto and was astonished to discover that operas had a *story*! Melodramatic maybe, but riveting nevertheless. I hungered for more. Wagner. Puccini. Verdi. Leoncavallo. Why didn't *everybody* get as excited as I did?

Antiques happened because I used to glue my nose to the window of a little antique shop in town, run by Tweedledum and Tweedledee. Two round little brothers, who were as cheerful as they were anachronistic. They invited me in. I liked a silver cream jug. They told me all about it: Made in Chester in 1765. They explained how to read hallmarks. I was fascinated. They offered to let me buy it by paying instalments.

So every Saturday I took a bus to town with my pocket money clutched in a sweaty hand, and placed it reverently in one of their pudgy paws.

The cream jug was followed by two forks by Paul Storr, 1819. A friend of Father's gave me a percussion rifle from 1859, which had been found on the bed of the Vaal River. In the mouldy wood and rusty iron I could hear the trapped voices of that old explorer, or trapper, or hunter, as he fell full of arrows, or assegais, or a heart attack. That was thrilling.

So I started collecting guns as well.

Weird.

It was not until I left high school to go to Cram College that my political involvement went beyond rows with classmates and occasional poster-sticking.

I explain. King George School and I did not get on. You will have gathered that. My last two years were turbulent. Teachers regarded me as a rebel because I succeeded in annoying every one of them, either in my role as newspaper editor (I managed to retain my editorship by promising to be Good. I wasn't) or class loony. My fellow-pupils regarded me as a weirdo because I espoused black freedom.

We came to the inevitable conclusion, King George and I, that we should part. The decision was made largely as a result of a one-way conversation with Brandie: 'Do you want to pass this year, boy?' 'Yes, sir.' 'Well I give you notice now. However good your exam proves to be, I will ensure that you fail.' While I had been *officially* chastised and forgiven for my transgression against him, he had never really forgiven me. So he had his revenge. Thank you, sir.

Mummy, I want to go to Cram College.

Deep discussions. I won.

Cram College: it sits in the grimy centre of Johannesburg where the dusty 'sixties skyscrapers sullenly overlook the frantic multi-coloured streets. The college was formed by Willie De Vries shortly after the war on educational principles which were revolutionary. Revolutionary cramming. For me it was paradise. We were allowed to wear our own clothes. Lessons were like lectures. We were treated like adults, called Mr or Miss by our lecturers. Unlike the King George bunch, these were no seedy academics. These were lean, well-dressed, keen-as-mustard, sharp-as-razor businesslike beings who Meant Every Word they said.

In return for this measure of freedom, we were expected to learn, and learn, and learn. No excuses accepted. But no canings.

The pupils were the throwouts of hundreds of white schools. Each was a rebel of a sort. There were boozers, druggies, gays, the intellectually lazy, the subnormal.

And.

Thrill of thrills. *GIRLS!*

Girls in tresses and dresses and make-up. Colourful, real. Ass. Tonishing.

So I fell in love. It was a breathless, choking thing. It caused sweaty hands and stuttering voice and great confusion. She was called Joanna.

Her terribly English name was just right. The blonde, bubbly little girl from Sloane Square, London, still retained her roses-with-thorns accent. She also had acres of personality, dressed vigorously, made up arrogantly, walked determinedly and led me on shamelessly. We met in the lift. Bzz, hummm, click! Third floor. Canteen.

Our exciting discovery of each other was doomed to stay on the intellectual plane. We discovered that we had everything in common. Except the bulges in our bodies, which were differently distributed. And for some reason she never let me explore her cracks and mounds.

A shame. We were both rebels, parent haters, Afrikaner haters, book lovers. But I couldn't screw a book. And boy, did I want to screw her!

Me sixteen and a virgin dying not to be one.

We got into the wicked habit of going to jazz clubs at night and getting stupid drunk. I would wait until the parents were out or asleep. Then I would climb out of the window with Mummy's spare keys, push the car out of the driveway, start it up and roar off toward Hillbrow.

Hillbrow was clubland, flatland, sexland. Garish, neon pavement cafés where all drugs were available, jazz clubs where progressive jazz would blare out to drunk, befuddled teenagers who would try to keep their feet still – tapping was 'uncool'. Yeh. Actually only my body is here the rest of me is up in Heaven with that sax. Yeh.

One night she got into the car breathless and said, 'Tonight we've got to see Jerry, OK?'

'Yes sure,' I said, heart beating, stomach churning – all the usual ills I suffered whenever she was near.

'Don't you want to know who Jerry is?' she giggled.

'No.' I said. Put the car into second gear and lurched off.

We met Celeste outside the club. 'We're going to see Jerry,' Joanna announced.

'Can I come?' Joanna was unsure but. OK.

We went to this little park on a hill in the middle of Hillbrow. Hillbrow's brow. Hairy eyebrow. He sat in the middle of a flower bed on the peonies. Joanna nudged me and grinned at my puzzle.

Jerry was a huge man in his fifties with a long grey beard and hair that lay dead on his shoulders. He smoked an incredible pipe. It was long, and red. The stem was a good curving eighteen inches and ended in a bowl which was carved into what looked like a self-portrait. When he sucked it bubbled. The smell of old socks and ammonia clung to his filthy clothes.

He looked like an old tramp. It took me many years to realise that was just what he was.

'Hallo umm,' he said. His voice was fruity, very English, deep and humorous.

'Hallo, Jerry,' Joanna answered. 'I've brought Celeste, and this is a new friend.'

'Oh hallo! Welcome.' He turned to Joanna. 'Does he rave?'

This was a very peculiar and intriguing question. Was he asking her if I was mad?

You see, Johannesburg was riddled at that time with Greenwich-Village style Beatniks. Dirty, jazz-mad, drink-worshipping, wild children of the night who lived in bare flats and broken-down houses where the cockroaches were treated as equals. They had their own language, stolen to a large extent from their American contemporaries, but with a distinct South African flavour. Their heroes were Ginsberg, Corso, Kerouac, Ferlinghetti. They called themselves Ravers, from the verb, to rave. This derived from their fondness for amphetamines. Which make you rave and rave, on and onandonandon. Jerry was asking Joanna whether I took drugs.

I thought he was asking her if I was completely potty, and probably took umbrage. I nevertheless thought it quite deep, and, in the darkness, with the lights of Johannesburg below, and the crushed peonies peeping out from under Jerry's bottom, it seemed as if I had been privileged to meet a Prophet, or Saint. At least a Guru.

Which was why, when he handed me a pipe smelling of ammonia and old socks, I accepted, and inhaled earnestly.

Everybody was acting very silly indeed. I didn't feel too silly myself, just a little happier than usual, nevertheless I displayed the headstands I had learnt from Mac many years before. One had to groove, man, go with the flow; the jargon puts my teeth on edge now.

That was the first time I smoked dagga. It wasn't the last, oh no, despite the fact that I felt nothing at all. Jerry later told me that one doesn't feel truly stoned until the fourth time. He called it 'scene four', to make it sound like a jazz tune, I suppose.

So I began to hang about the incredible little base-ment room he inhabited. I think he regarded me as a disciple, which was what I wanted, and after a while he made me my own pipe: the final sign of acceptance.

One of the results of my new interest in grass was meeting a lot of black people. They were the source of most of the grass in Johannesburg. Our gardener very kindly grew a huge bush of marijuana in my parents' back garden. Unfortunately, the new dog, a cocker spaniel called Mr Magoo, discovered that he liked the taste of the leaves a great deal. Was he once Thomas De Quincey? Whether or not, he spent a lot more time stoned and giggling about the place than I did.

He could sit watching Mother playing bridge for hours. The Bridge Game was a very special occasion for the rich Northern Suburb Jewish ladies. Four prim, perfectly groomed women, each looking five to six-and-a-half years younger than her true age, dressed in Saint Laurent and smelling very expensive indeed. The maid brought tea and biscuits. The ladies played and gossiped and carefully evaluated their partners' and opponents' dresses, jewellery, make-up.

One day Mr Magoo was so absorbed in a brilliant exchange of bidding that he forgot to go outside to pee and casually let it all go on Gertie Kaplan's leg.

This was a fatal mistake, and he died in mysterious circumstances two days later. Whether Mother had put arsenic in his Yum Yums or whether he had an over-dose of grass, I will never know.

Mr Magoo was furious, as he never got to see the return match.

I keep trying to tell you about how I got myself more deeply into politics.

It happened this way: My meetings with black people (albeit usually in pursuit of drugs), the influence of my parents' remote liberalism, my whole orientation, had made me acutely aware of the injustices around me.

A VAGUE MEMORY OF THE LAST MEETING OF THE LIBERAL PARTY

The Liberal Party of South Africa was the last inter-racial party in the country. The Government brought in a law whereby 'Different Races' were prohibited from 'interfering' with other races' politics. This meant, effectively, that multi-racial parties were banned.

The hall was packed with all colours. We felt as if a cloud had appeared in the room, and if we didn't hurry up, we'd all be caught by the storm.

I remember the air of misery and defeat as the speakers made their farewell speeches. They had no intention of making the party mono-racial. There was no choice but to disband.

The meeting was to ravage my ravaged life. Not because of all that, but because of this: The person sitting next to me was a very good-looking young Coloured fellow who, from his muttered responses, was unusually articulate. So, after the ritual singing of 'We Shall Overcome', which sounded like Lincoln trying to sing with Booth's bullet deep in his brain, I invited him to join me for a coffee.

This was not a practical proposition, as at that time no persons of Colour could drink coffee – or anything else – in a 'white' coffee-bar. So after an embarrassing incident at Chesa's, he invited me to his place, which was a linoleumed white-painted shrine of a room in a ramshackle Fordsburg building, not far from Stones' Hotel.

Fordsburg is the older, poorer part of Johannesburg, the down-market equivalent of Parktown. It is dominated by the hotel, which towers over the mess like a Victorian dowager in a soup kitchen. Fordsburg consists largely of run-down bungalows with tiny yards, peeling paint, corrugated-iron roofs. Stoeps run all around the houses, which are inhabited by Coloured and Indian families, dogs, rats and fleas, dagga dealers, dust, grime and crime in symbiotic harmony. This was Darryl's home, the pit from which he had emerged.

He was an intense, ambitious and well-educated young man who worked in a Christian bookshop in town. He had been brought up and educated by monks and his attitude to life was littered with their prejudices.

He read James Baldwin, Luther King, listened to operettas and was as sincere as toast.

So we drank dreadful coffee with condensed milk, listened to Gilbert and Sullivan, and played the 'Ain't it awful?' game and 'What a pity everybody isn't as clever as us'.

I felt awfully self-righteous sitting there with him – in *Fordsburg*, as well! Though I couldn't understand why he didn't rave. Something to do with Jesus, I suppose, and the lack of evidence concerning His indulgence in Substances.

I started to visit Darryl regularly, though after a while it became less pleasure, more duty. The Problems: I couldn't invite him home, I couldn't predict how Mapa (my collective term for the parents) would react. Beside wot wld the neighbours say and stuff like that. We couldn't go to movies together. We couldn't go out for a meal. We couldn't even sit in a bus together. The odd couple.

So I'd go there. We'd talk. That was legal, within limits. All we could do.

About this time I nearly got myself thrown out of college.

Me and some girls decided to produce a newspaper. The purpose of the newspaper, which would be given away free, was simply to print statistics, facts about the South African situation, with extracts from the Institute of Race Relations reports (which contained facts like the discrepancy in education spending between Black and White which I have mentioned), Hansard (to show how absurd and narrow-minded our politicians were – all without comment. Just the facts. We were naive enough to believe that if people had the *facts*, they couldn't continue to support a Government which acted so unfairly. . .

Alas, people don't really care about fairness. They're more interested in money and bombs and babies and tax.

We had these meetings, in which we declared ourselves to be a Bond of Brothers (a liberal Broederbond?) and had we thought of it, we would probably have had a Bloodbrother ceremony as well. We talked and talked and talked. Planned. Collected subscriptions from each other. Swore secrecy.

Then one day Dr De Vries, the College Principal, summoned me to his office.

'Sit down please, Mr Bloch.'

'Hallo.'

'Um. I had a visit the other day.'

'Oh yes—'

He took his glasses off and wiped them with a virulently red handkerchief.

Dr De Vries was a delightfully pudgy man with a wispy moustache, balding, in his fifties. He usually smoked cigars, but there were none in evidence today. He was edgy, trying to cut down on smoking.

He usually behaved toward us like a benevolent dictator, whose pockets contained both sweets and hand-grenades.

We liked him, but no one loved him.

'What are your politics, Bloch?'

'That's a very personal question, Doctor.'

'Look.' He glints. I'm not used to him glinty. 'I am being Very Serious, and you will be Very Serious.'

A pause as I digest this. I grow serious. 'Yes, sir?'

'Don't call me Sir! You know I don't like it.' This is

the first time I have heard him raise his voice, ever. I am now very worried. 'I have just had a visit from the Security Branch.'

OK, you win. I am now sweating, heart pumping, it feels like being with Joanna but not so nice. 'Yes—?'

'Yes. The subject under discussion was you.'

Aha, my chance for martyrdom. On the other hand, maybe martyrdom hurts. 'What did they say?'

'They said, young man, that you might be a Communist.'

'Aha.' Pause, then, 'I'm not a Communist.'

'How do I know that, Mr Bloch?'

'I'm *telling* you! I'm not a Communist. I have never even *read* Marx!'

'Don't shout at me and calm down. If you are not a Communist, why are you running a Secret Society?' His hands seek the ghost of a cigar in an empty box.

'Oh no!'

'So you *are* running a Secret Society?'

'It's not – I mean, we're not doing anything illegal—'

'Don't tell me what you are doing. I don't want to know. You know what else they said?'

'What?'

'They said if I don't stop you they'll close down the college.'

'They can't do that – on what grounds?'

'They don't need grounds. Don't you know what country you're living in? You're playing a very dangerous game.' He is standing now, leaning on the desk, pointing his nose at me like a pistol. 'And you're playing it with *my* living, *my* life. I want you to stop it.'

'But—'

'I don't want buts. I want you to agree to stop it.'

'I can't—'

'Don't say can't. Never say can't. You can and will stop it. Or I'll expel you, and you can be someone else's problem.'

'I see.'

'Goodbye for now, Bloch.'

'Goodbye, sir.'

But it wasn't goodbye. How could I continue with the society when it was obvious that there was an informer amongst us? *Someone* talked to the Security Branch, and it wasn't me. So I disbanded the Secret Society and passed my Matriculation exam (university entrance) instead.

Darryl and I came up with a Brilliant Plan. We would go on holiday together, to Moçambique, multi-racial Moçambique. We could stay in the same hotel, go to movies together, swim on the same beach! He had a shiny little Mini which would carry our multi-racial bodies there, no hassle. Problem? No problem.

Mapa, I want to go on holiday.

'Fine, darling,' says Mummy, doling peas on to the plate. Seaton, the houseboy, holds the plate awkwardly in one hand, ready to make his unsteady way around the table to my seat. He is very drunk. 'Where do you want to go?'

'I was thinking of Lourenço Marques.'

She adds mashed potatoes to the plate, which looks ready to tip.

'Don't think you're going alone,' Father growls. He is in his usual pale, nerve-wracked state, Hard Day at the Office.

Plowsky kicks Michelle under the table. 'He's *kicking* me, Mommy.'

'No problem,' I decide to be casual. 'A friend is going with me.'

'Who, darling? – Barry, stop that.' She drops two lamb chops on the plate and it lurches off on its dangerous journey.

'His name is Darryl. I don't think you know him.

Thank you, Seaton.' (His name wasn't Seaton. It was Silva, he was a Portuguese-Moçambiquan Black and was working there illegally. Mother decided to call him Seaton because it didn't sound as *foreign* as Silva, because Seaton sounded awfully butlerish and because saying 'Clean the silver, Silva,' would have been silly.)

'Isn't that the *Coloured* boy you have been visiting?'

Thanks, Mum, you've betrayed me yet again, I must learn not to tell you anything. 'Um. Yes.'

Father has emerged into Full Alert. 'You are NOT going on holiday with that boy.'

'Why not?'

'Don't ask me why not!' Silva steps back, the better to view the proceedings. He knows, from experience, that these rows can cause the launch of objects never designed for flying. 'On NO account are you going.' He's started to spray. Always a bad sign.

'That's ridiculous. He's—'

'Calm down, dear.' Mother tries to mediate. 'If your father says you can't go, you can't go.' She motions impatiently to Seaton to resume serving. He's leaning against the sideboard and has serious doubts about going anywhere.

'I don't believe what I'm *hearing*!' ('Mummy, he's kicking me again!') 'What's wrong with Darryl?'

'Don't ask stupid questions.' A whole pea escapes Father's mouth and enters the runny butter in an attempt to hide from its inevitable doom.

'You claim to be so *liberal*, damn it, you won't let me go on holiday with him because he's Coloured!'

'It's nothing to do with that. Jesus, you're so stupid! You will do what I tell you.' Father is extraordinarily riled, out of control almost.

'That just proves what I've always known. You're a bunch of hypocrites. How can you claim to want equal rights for Blacks and—'

'Shut up and leave the table!'

I stand. 'Father, I'm telling you, I am old enough to make my *own* decisions. I am going and that's all there is to it.'

'Old enough, are you? OLD enough?' He's standing too. Seaton gapes from what he thinks may be a safe distance. 'You're not old enough to avoid me giving you a bloody good hiding!' He dashes round the table at me, knocking Seaton and a plate of lamb chops and veg flying.

To his surprise I don't run: wait there for him. He grabs me by the shoulders. Mother screams. I catch him with an uppercut. He falls, not unconscious but shaken. Tries to rise. I hit him again. Tries to rise. I hit him again hit him again. Mother begs *please*. Plowsky shouts, 'Hit him again.' 'Daddy!' Michelle screams.

Father is gasping between blows, 'You weakling, you can't even hurt me.'

I am not trying to hurt him. I'm just trying to keep him down so he doesn't get up and *kill* me. Biff biff biff.

Then I dash to my room and start to pack.

Their bedroom door slams. They argue for a while then Mother comes out, knocks gently on my door. Come in.

'What are you doing?' She closes the door after her.

'I'm packing, Mother. I'm leaving.'

She sits wearily on the bed. 'Don't be silly, darling.'

'I'm not being silly. I've finished school. Why should I stay here?'

She sighs. 'It may not seem like it sometimes, but we love you, darling.'

'Har bloody har.' I decide the fluffy pullover is better than the Gucci one.

'You must understand, darling, your father can't let you go.'

'I don't understand, how *can* I understand.' I throw my underwear on to the bed. Crisply ironed Y-fronts, crisply ironed socks.

'Well, darling, if you don't understand *now*—'

'Mother, please listen to me. I hate him so much. And he has hated me since – ever since – always. There's only bad feeling between us. I can't share this roof with him.'

She straightens the piled underwear. I snatch it and crush it into the case. 'Look, darling, I can't take this,' her eyes are moistening. Oh no, not that. 'Why don't you just go for a nice little walk or something? You'll feel better.'

'Don't be so *patronising*. I'm perfectly calm. I have made the obvious, logical decision. When faced with an impossible situation, the only reasonable thing to do is run away, right? Don't cry, Mum.' I can't drape the arm over the shoulders, which is what she wants me to do. Waves of I-Want-Comfort pour out. But who got me into this? Who betrayed me?

'He'll send the Police after you.'

'I don't care if he sends the *Army*!' I bang the case shut. Click the locks, click click. Committed now. Whether I will or no. I gotta go. Oh shit. 'They won't find me.'

'Wait,' she says, and thrusts two five-rand notes into my hand. 'Take these. Phone me when you want to come home.'

'Never. Goodbye.' A melodramatic swishing of a cloak would have been appropriate here. But I didn't have one.

'Kiss me goodbye, Tom.'

Peck.

She stands there forlorn on the front step. Michelle peers at my departing back hoping she'll never see me again. Plowsky shouts through the window 'Come back, you idiot.'

I bang the garden gate, tomb closing, down the road, a lonely confused little dog wuffs at my ankles as I go down the street, then goes home to a nice warm doggie box.

It took me years to discover why Father had been so frightened about my getting so het up about black people.

If I had known then what I know now. Clichés like that should be banned, they cause so much sorrow.

Five

'When I was in America,' said Umfaan, 'my name was Joe, and I was a friend of the greatest gangsters in a town called New Orleans.'

'Don't tell me that, Umfaan. How could a South African be a gangster in New Orleans?' Pieter had grown a good deal since we last met him in his short pants and face fuzz.

Now he shaves, and has incredible blue eyes and shocking, uncontrollable blond hair. It's not the dead shiny stuff Scandinavians grow, it's rather more wavy than that and grows every which way above the short back and sides, the slightly too-big ears God, who has a sense of humour, landed him with.

He has become more sceptical, and between those ears he keeps a mind that crackles with questions and answers, and his propensity for independent thinking worries his schoolmasters who cannot force it into their own narrow world-view.

Umfaan had taught Pieter to think. Most important, he taught the boy to question everything he was told, especially by teachers, parents, schoolmates. And, of course, Umfaan.

The Art of Mercuriality Explained

By Professor U. Mareta Wena Hao, BA, LLB, BLit, MRCP

When I was in America, my name was Joe, and I was a friend of the greatest gangsters in a town called New Orleans.

The Government had declared the purchase, sale and imbibing of alcoholic liquor to be illegal. Why did they make it illegal when everybody except a handful of mad Christians liked it so much? Ask our own Government, my boy, for they think we Blacks are so childish that it is illegal for us too. It is *very* funny when you remember that *even* Jesus turned water into wine. I think the whole thing, in America at any rate, was a plot by Organised Crime who could make far greater profits from something that is banned than from something that anyone can buy at the corner shop.

So I decided to make my fortune by becoming involved in this lucrative business.

In New Orleans there were many what they called, speakeasies. These were the shebeens of that town where anybody could go and get a drink or a girl or a bit of dagga. Every now and then the police would raid a place and shut it down. A few weeks later it would open up again.

I became a runner. This meant that I would take a truck in dead of night to a secret location where people in masks loaded crates of Scotch whisky on to my truck, drink which had just crossed the *whole* Atlantic Ocean in crates labelled 'Hairdressing Tonic' to be there with me!

Oh yes, I only dealt in the best! Good imported whisky, none of this backyard rubbish we make here for the black people.

Then I would drive to the farm of a friend called Willie Martin. There we carefully unloaded the crates.

Opened them. Expertly prised open the bottles. Added one third water. Poured the extra whisky, plus water, into empty bottles we had been collecting and sealed them all so *no one* would know they had ever been opened. Repack the crates. I would deliver them, as ordered, to Macready.

Later, I would sell the other bottles to other customers, and Willie and I would pocket the profits.

If Macready had known he would have had my balls for breakfast.

A good scam, né Pietie? But life doesn't like good scams and is always trying to find ways to destroy the best laid plans.

Now, Willie had a wife. This is a problem many men have had throughout history. And she fancied me *very* much.

(Was Willie and his wife white, Umfaan?)

(What's that got to do with it?)

(Nothing, Umfaan. Go on.)

She was a willowy little thing, about four feet nothing high with long blonde hair—

(Caught you. She *was* white.)

(Draw your own conclusions.)

—but believe me she had the greatest set of titties you have ever seen. Au!

When I used to come there she would stand and watch Willie and me at work. But she wasn't watching Willie, she was looking at me. Her eyes stroked my bared forearms, my strong chest, my tight stomach, my crotch where they lingered, asking the question Is it true what they say about black men?

(Is it true what they say about black men, Umfaan?)

(Haw, haw!)

This went on for six months. Once a week I made this dangerous journey and worked there in Willie's dangerous barn and was pawed by his wife's dangerous eyes.

Suddenly one night Willie wasn't there.

Winnie greeted me like an old friend. 'Hi Joe, you're late.'

'There was a roadblock,' I said. 'I had to use another route. Where's Willie?'

'Oh heck, he's been sampling last week's consignment. He's fast asleep in the house.'

This was *very* strange, I found it hard to believe. Business always came first with Willie. Nevermind, I took a deep breath and my heart started to bump in my chest and my forehead and armpits were wet. 'Well,' I said trying to pull myself together, 'we'd better get on with the work. Do you know how to do it?'

She stared me straight in the eyes. 'Of course I know how to do it. Do you?' She was also breathing too hard and her breasts were trying to escape the heart thumping behind them. I could see the nipples pointing at me, beckoning my hands.

'Yes,' I said, and without receiving any orders my hands leapt to her blouse and tried to attach themselves to her nipples.

'Wait,' she said breathless. 'Let's go to the bed! Come on. Quickly!'

She took me to the dark farmhouse, and into the bedroom. There in the moonlight – there was no electricity – I could see the big snoring form of my friend, like the bulge in the stomach of the python who has swallowed a springbok.

'Don't worry,' she whispered. 'I put this in his drink and he won't wake up till morning.' She showed me a bottle of brown powder. 'Come *on*,' she said. 'I want to make it with you. Here. Next to Willie.' So I did.

Au! She knew how to satisfy a man and she found an answer to her Question.

After, we were lying there in the bed, each thinking our own things, when she said, 'Joe, I don't think he's breathing.'

'What?'

'Willie,' she said. 'Is he breathing?'

Well, I put my ear to his mouth and nose. Silent. I turned him over and it was like turning a dead whale. 'Oh God!' she screamed when she realised the awful truth. 'I must have given him too much. What shall we do?'

'Phew,' I said, thinking of the delayed consignment. 'Now we're in trouble.'

We discussed for hours, and I came up with the only plan that would work. So simple!

We dashed back to the barn. There, with perfect co-operation, we carried out the dilution operation on the whisky. Then we loaded the consignment on to the truck and went back to the house where we covered Willie all over with the juice of the kwanga nut mixed with brown clothes dye. When we were finished, we had made a black man. A dead black man.

We dressed him in my clothes and put him on to the truck. Then, with her following in Willie's pickup, we drove round the corner from the roadblock.

We put Willie in the driving seat, jammed his foot on the throttle, pointed the truck at the roadblock and drove like hell back to the farm!

Next day the headlines said, 'Boozerunner Shot at Roadblock. Scotch Whisky seized'. So I was safe from Macready's boys – Joe was dead, as far as the world was concerned. And I became a respectable Louisiana farmer, married to the loveliest pair of breasts in the County.

'How could you suddenly become a white farmer, Umfaan? I don't believe—'

'You haven't been listening, boy. Realise this: no one sees what you *are*, they see what they *expect* to see. People put labels on people, like: Farmer, White, Good Ole Boy. Or dumbell, black, useless. Or boy, white, Too Many Questions.

'So I could easily become Farmer, White, Good Ole

Boy with only a wig and a little application of a proprietary skin dye sold to black folks who wanted to look more white.

'You must understand this: I *became* Willie Martin. I believed everything he believed. I loved his wife. I tilled his fields.

'And the man who crashed into that roadblock riddled with bullets *was* Joe, the dumcluck Black who thought he could drive his illegal load straight through twenty fully armed State Troopers and thirteen murderous cops.'

Pieter laughed heartily. 'And how long did you keep up this farce?'

'Till I died of old age, you stupid!'

Pieter discovered sex and it was like falling into the sea and finding it to be freezing cold. At first you want to scream and get out. Then the body adjusts and you begin to enjoy it.

His first experience was at the Pandokkies, and Umfaan had something to do with it.

One day he came there and Umfaan was sitting under the tree as usual. Pieter had just finished his English exam, and expected high marks. He had written a story about drink-running in New Orleans during Prohibition for his essay.

He had come to tell Umfaan about it, what a clever boy he was et cetera.

'What do you want?' Umfaan said gruffly. 'I'm busy with the *amadhlozi*.' He threw some brown bones and beads on to a sacred rug and studied the configurations.

'What's the matter with you today, Umfaan? I have come to visit you.'

'Shut up, let me . . . ah. Stupid Mevrou Van Rensburg is pregnant again. Birth death birth death.'

'I don't believe you.'

110

'Quiet. Why do you steal my story?'

'I didn't steal it. You gave it to me.'

'That's true,' said Umfaan, returning to the bones.

'How can somebody who has travelled everywhere and done everything believe in all this superstitious rubbish?'

'How can all this superstitious rubbish know you'd stolen my story?'

'That's true too.' Pieter laughed. 'What's the sense in my telling you everything if you know it all already?'

'It's all rubbish anyway,' Umfaan said, and gathered the bones into the cloth. 'You have to go inside now. Selina is waiting for you.'

'Why?'

'Don't ask questions. There's a present for you inside, for passing your exams.'

'I don't know I've passed yet.'

'I do,' grinned the skellum.

Selina was stirring a brew of meat and leaves in a pot on the iron stove. A chubby little girl sat on a broken chair watching her and grinning.

'Hey, Selina,' Pieter hugged her (he never hugged his mother), 'how's my favourite antique?' He always called her his antique. She thought he was saying Auntie.

'O my Pietie, you are very welcome. Do you want some soup?' She extracted herself from his arms.

The fat girl giggled. 'Who's this baasie, Selina? Is this your boyfriend?'

'Don't be rude, Mifi. This is my Pietie. Ibroughthimup. You must excuse this girl, Pietie, she is my niece from the township. They have no manners there.'

'You're from the city?' Piet asked. He had never seen a city.

'Yes, baasie. I live in Daveyton Township, it's by Benoni.'

'Benoni is a big city, is it?'

'It's not so big as Johannesburg, but much bigger

than Ventersdaal, baas,' she said, eyes lowered.

'This is not a baas,' said Selina. 'This is my boyboy, my Pietie. You can call him Pietie. Have something to eat, my boy.'

'You can't feed him that dogsbrew!' Selina has given her licence to abandon the accepted black-white norms.

'He *likes* my stew. I use only good meat in this. Ai! You have no manners, really.' Selina had carefully selected the most gristlefree bits of meat for the stew, knowing Piet was coming.

'Selina!' Umfaan was calling outside. 'Come here I want you!'

With a sigh that said What does the old man want now, what a nuisance, she bustled out.

The young people sat there and tried to act naturally while each appraised the other. Hm, Piet thought, she's not so young after all, maybe thirty. It's just that being fat the age lines don't show.

Hm, Mifi thought, he's not so bad but what a pity he's pale, and so scrawny. I wonder if he has freckles on his shoulders like the teacher I visit in Benoni.

'It's very hot here,' Piet said.

'Yes.'

His body hair must be all yellow as well but at least he doesn't have a bup, I can see that from here.

She's got great big breasts, I must remember them for later.

He's quite a tall boy, I suppose he has a little one. Hau, to come all this way for a little one. And do I get paid? Forget it! Umfaan is meaner with money than a Jew.

'What work do you do there?' Piet's eyes stray to the stew which is boiling furiously.

'I am a cleaner, in the town hall.' This is the standard story she tells inquisitive Whites. It is the story in her pass.

Well, why doesn't he get on with it? I hate these talkers, they waste my time.

Why is Selina so long? I want my eats.

'Do you like it in Benoni?'

I like 'it' anywhere. 'Yes, it's very nice.' Oh hell, he's a virgin. Why didn't the old bastard tell me?

Where is Selina? That stew will be dry. Why must I sit here? I'd rather be talking to Umfaan.

Pieter stood with an unspoken 'Well . . .'

'Where are you going?' Mifi was startled. What's he doing now?

'Um – I thought I'd go outside and tell Selina the stew—'

'Nevermind the stew! Are you going to do it or not? I don't have all day!'

'What . . . ?'

'They are waiting for us to finish. Come on, sex now, stew later. Come here!' Mifi was completely in control of the situation. She had long ago discovered that the only time you could give a white man orders was when you were in a sex situation with him.

'You mean, you want— Umfaan! He expects— I'll kill him!'

'All right, when you've finished killing him I will too. Nevermind.' She barred the doorway. 'First, kiss me.'

'I don't want to.'

She cupped a hand over his crotch and that was it. 'What's this? What's this between your legs?' His resistance shrank, his dick grew. No control. Mind of its own. Nevermind.

Her hand gently manipulated the growing bulge. 'I think I've found a little animal,' she teased, giggling coyly. 'A little animal! Wants to come out to play!'

'Oh no . . .'

'Little kitty cat! Stroke the little kitty cat, see how it purrs?'

'Oh no . . .'

'Little cat flap, open the little cat flap, yehr, all those silly buttons, yehr . . .'

It popped out, curious little head – 'Who's disturbing

113

the great sleeping trouser snake?' Came face to face with a set of opened lips, cooing, nibbling, expertly tweaking into wakefulness and HOW, tongue escapes to explore the veins of it and the Slurp! halfway down a throat endless passageway of pleasure Not YET! Not YET! mouth withdraws and a deep gaping hairlined smile throbs, invites, GLOMP! In in in . . . inoutinout-inoutinout . . .

Bang, crash, the Philharmonia plays the *1812* and all the cannons go of at ONCE! Puff pant puff pant. Whew!

So this is what it's like to not be a virgin. It's pretty tacky. Sweats like hell.

Is that *all*? Well, how can I expect a virgin to understand that I need a climax too. I wonder if I can get him going again.

Selina bust her way in. 'My stew, my stew! *Why* you didn't take it off the stove before?'

'Umfaan, WHY did you do that to me? I could *kill* you!'

'Now, *what* did I do?'.

'That – you know—'

'Oh ho ho ho!'

'I've broken the law—'

'Have you?'

'Don't be so bloody smug, you—'

'Shut up a minute. You are treading old ground.'

'What do you mean?'

'Before your mother came along, where do you think your father spent his free time?'

'I don't understand—'

'Go away and think about it.'

Gosh, it's taken me 111 pages to get to the sex. That's because there wasn't any before. Well, hardly any.

When I ran away I was still a virgin. Well, almost. I had never placed my warm willie in a woman. This caused me a great deal of anxiety at the time. After all, I had tried to lose my virginity often enough. Once I had even managed to put my hand inside Joanna's knickers but she had been frightened and withdrawn her thighs so suddenly that I had felt hurt and confused.

Rejection, the teenager's nightmare.

Absolom had, of course, had plenty of sex but it was a very minor part of his life. There had been township women by the score, I suppose. There was even a white liberal madam who had made the final sacrifice. But Absolom had spent a great deal of his life in prison. This often leads to desperate experiments with other men.

Not in Absolom's case. He was too much in love with his destiny for that. When he was arrested in 1961, he was kept separate from other prisoners, for fear he would infect them with Communism.

In any case, the police didn't want anyone to see what a mess they had made of him. They were still smarting from the defeat inflicted on them by the South African courts, when 156 leaders of the Congress movement were acquitted of high treason. They wanted to arrest all Communists. Torture them. Kill them if possible.

But they couldn't kill Molapo. He was luckier than so many of the others, who were squashed by the system, bruised, ripped, broken – then allowed to 'fall down stairs' or 'commit suicide'. Absolom suffered in those first three months as much as any of these. Then he confessed.

One

'On the Road Again', doo be doo, on the road again, led by the thumb across the wasted, hate-torn country humming insanely, thinking of Kerouac. Dylan. Wearing an American accent like a cloak. 'Yeh,' I would say with complete conviction to my purveyors of free lifts, 'my name is Chuck (that's American for Charles, you know) Greenberg, and I come from Barrington Rhode Island USA.'

'Jees,' they would reply, 'and what do you think of our great country?'

'Very nice,' I would say and wish the ride were over.

Hitchhiking is another world. These are the rules:

1. Agree with everything the liftor says
2. Be whatever the liftor wants you to be
3. Tell him how hard it will be to get a lift from wherever he wants to drop you, in the hope that he will extend his journey
4. Suggest that you may be hungry
5. At all costs, be bright, cheerful, and of course, GRATEFUL.

Chuck Greenberg, by the way, was an American exchange student whose personality I adopted completely. There was no chink in my armour. I believed in the role. If Father had indeed reported my 'disappearance' to the police, not one of my liftors would credit that the young man who had ridden in their car was a teenage rebel from Johannesburg's Northern Suburbs who had beaten up his father and split.

My lifts were from: A truckdriver who insisted that I keep talking to stop him falling asleep. After two hours I had run out of Greenberg stories, and though my accent held out it became pretty ragged. It was good practice nevertheless. When he let me out I slept in a men's room at a service station in Harrismith.

The next guy was a red-faced farmer called McKenzie, who had come to South Africa in 1939, because 'They know how to deal with Blacks here.'

'Great,' I said. 'Sure, you guys should look at what the US did to the Indians. You could learn a lot.'

'Huh?'

'First we peppered them with gunshot, then we infected them with smallpox. Great, huh?'

'Right!'

An Afrikaans drug rep was the next victim. He demanded stories about the Old West, knew every movie John Wayne had made, asked me if I had ever met him ('Sure!'), showed me his revolver.

This nightmare lasted to Estcourt.

Next: The English headmaster of a church school near Pietermaritzburg. He was my greatest challenge. He was an intelligent, committed Christian, bright-faced and cheery and his questions were penetrating. We discussed the differences between schools in the USA and South Africa. I had to search my memory desperately for everything Chuck had told me.

By the time we reached Pietermaritzburg I was fraying at the edges, and grateful that the ordeal was almost over.

Then, as he dropped me by the town hall, he said, 'You know, I have an idea. How would you like to come to the school with me? You can sleep at our house tonight, we'll give you a good meal and in the morning you can give my boys a lecture.'

Me, aghast, 'What about?'

'Well, you could tell us all about the United States' view of South Africa.'

'I'm, uh – not very good at speaking, I really don't think—'

'Look, if you do I promise to find you a lift to Durban, all the way. Come on, say yes.'

'I—'

'Tell you what. I have to do some shopping. I'll be a couple of hours. I'll be back here at two. If you decide to come, be here to meet me.'

'Right. Thanks for the offer. I'll um— . . . '

And I had doubted that he'd been taken in.

I wandered about a bit. Bought a sandwich with my dwindling rands. No, I couldn't do it. But hunger. Nah. But night would be happening soon and. Surely no. And a lift all the way to Durban would be very nice. Huh? And a warm bed and clean sheets. Oh hell. And chicken. And roast potatoes.

Wot the hell. So I did it.

He had a charming wife who made excellent roast potatoes and kept their pine-furnitured house Vim-clean and Johnson's-wax shiny. They had two pretty blond kids who weren't precocious, just clever. And there was a lovely soft bed in the guest room with clean sheets which, after a bath, gave me a powerful sleep.

119

Address by Mr C. Greenberg of the USA to the School

The School is gathered in the Assembly Hall. It's a boys' school, and they are all there in the pine pews in their black blazers and striped ties. Their shirts are whiter than those of my school-fellows. Even their teeth are whiter. Teachers line the back row.

They sing a hymn ('All things bright and beautiful'), then it's my turn.

'I would like to thank Mr Wilson, your Headmaster, for inviting me here and for his hospitality.

'He has asked me to talk to you about the American View of South Africa. As an exchange student, I have been here for a year. This gives me a rather different view to that of most of my countrymen.

'When I told my friends I was going to South Africa, they asked me, "Where's that?" ' (Titters) 'Which is a kinda funny question when you consider that only South Africa, Northern Ireland and a couple of other countries have been so unoriginal as to name their countries after their geographical location.

'There *are* Americans who know a little more about South Africa. There are Americans who know a great deal about your country. But however much they know, there are things they cannot understand.'

Right. Give it to them, Chuck.

'Few Americans would believe that seventy-five per cent of a population can be without a vote. We have a Constitution in the United States which guarantees these basic rights to all our people.

'We are puzzled by the fact that your Government has granted this huge majority their own so-called "states", consisting of the most barren thirteen per cent of the country.

'We do not understand why your black people have hardly any state money spent on their education.

120

'We find it incomprehensible that so many books are banned here. Like *Othello*. Can it really be true?

'To us, the concept of detention without trial is as foreign as Communist Russia.

'So the answer to the question, "What do Americans think about South Africa?" is, they just don't understand.

'Thank you.'

Stunned silence. I sure hit them with it. Or did I forget the accent? Oh dear, I feel as if I've been ungrateful or something.

'Any questions?' a bemused headmaster asks.

An elderly male teacher stands. He is red in the face. 'It's all very well for you! Don't you know that our Blacks have a higher standard of living than Blacks anywhere else in Africa?'

'Yes, that's because South Africa is the richest country in Africa. What I want to know is, why can't the Blacks have the same opportunity to take part in the running of your country as they have in mine?'

'You were right when you said you Americans just don't understand.' He's getting really mad now – at least two shades redder. 'What about the rest of Africa? Have you seen the mess the Blacks make of things when they're allowed to run their own countries?'

'Why does that surprise you? The borders were drawn by occupying colonial powers. They go right through tribal lands, cutting some in half and putting tribes who hate each other in the same damn countries.'

'Aha! That's what we are trying to do here. That's what Apartheid is about. Keeping tribes apart. *Now* do you understand, you arrogant little—'

'What, on thirteen per cent of the land? What's fair about that?'

We lob these grenades at each other over the heads of the delighted boys. The exchange is accompanied by showers of spit. It is beginning to get nasty.

'Oh yes, and have you seen the *cars* our Blacks drive? Have you seen their flashy *suits*? How dare you come here and criticise—'

'It's people like you who will be first up against the wall when the Revolution comes.'

'You see?' he shrieks at the boys. 'He's a Communist agitator! Let me at him!' He starts a crashing, boy-scattering progress toward the podium. Wilson grabs me by the arm and rushes me to the house.

He is apologetic. 'I'm sorry. He's normally quite a reasonable sort of chap.'

'I'm sorry too,' I say, and I was.

'There's something else I have to tell you I'm sorry about.'

'Oh?'

'He – Mr Callum – is supposed to be driving you to Durban.'

'Oh. Ha ha. Well.'

'Look, don' worry. I'll sort it out.' And he exits, practising his Christian goodwill smile.

I pack the pyjamas into the case. Wait. Should I vanish?

He comes bustling back. Triumph from ear to ear. 'He's calmed down now. Loves a good argument, he says. Are you ready?'

'Oh yes,' with trepidation.

'But before you go, promise me one thing.'

'What?'

'Write to me in five years' time and tell me if you still don't believe in God. Promise?'

'All right, but—'

I didn't write to him then, so I'm doing so now. Dear Mr Wilson, I'm sorry I deceived you all those years ago. I hope you're still alive and will somehow be able to get a banned copy of this. Yes, I do now believe in God. But less trammelled than your version. God is an Alien from the planet Xichra. He planted the earth garden so that he could farm it. For meat. His name is Karma. He was killed in 1975 by a number 37 bus in Clapham, South London, on his way to pick up a particularly good haunch of Cockney.

This was a story told to my friend Pieter by Umfaan, and is all lies. As everything said about God is. Except for His Name. Which is Karma.

Two

Umfaan's History of the World
I   The Old Testament

'When I was kidnapped by a space ship from the planet Xichra, I was a very small boy and—'

'Oh come on, Umfaan! As you get older your stories get sillier. Tell me a *true* story.'

'There's no such thing as a true story. Tell me, Pieter, is it true that God is in his Heaven and all's right with the world?'

'Of course it's true.'

'You see? That's rubbish. I can prove it to you.'

'Go on, then, I dare you.' Pieter settled himself on the dusty ground and lit a cigarette. The sun was trying to leave South Africa in search of more comfortable lands. It was leaving behind brilliant pink trails and gilded clouds. These too it would drag after itself eventually.

'When I was kidnapped by a space ship from the planet Xichra, I was a very small boy. I was also very stupit – my mother told me that every day. She said, "Umfaan, you are so stupid I'm surprised you don't wear your ears the wrong way round." This was in the Northern Transvaal, not far from here, in Pietersburg.

See? Even then they had named a town after you.

'I was playing in the mealie field on that day, when this man comes up and says, "Umfaan, I want you to come with me."

' "Yes, baas," I said. I called him Baas, though he wasn't a white man. He was a kind of purplish colour, with green stripes like a zebra.'

'Ha!' said Pieter.

'No, listen. But he was dressed very smartly in a perfectly cut suit, with a pink shirt and a tasteful green tie which matched his skin exactly. This was why I called him Baas.

'He led me by the hand to a dusty old Ford truck, which was covered in dents. We drove down the road out of sight to everybody, and the truck took off.

'Don't grin like that, if you'd seen that thing fly you wouldn't laugh. One minute we were going bump bump down a dirt track, then the earth just vanished and everything around us was black.

' "I hope you don't mind being kidnapped like this, Umfaan," the Baas said. "It's like this, I need some assistance for a little while. It's plenty lonely around this part of the galaxy. You understand, don't you?"

' "Yes, baas," I said.

' "Don't call me Baas," he said. "My name is Karma. You can call me Baas Karma."

' "Yes, Baas Karma."

' "Now be quiet. I have to concentrate on getting this bloody thing into the ship."

'Suddenly there was a huge silver object in front of us. It was shaped like a salami. As we came nearer, I saw that what had looked like a black spot from a distance was a door, open, and the Ford pickup flew straight in.

'It closed behind us, and the Baas breathed a sigh of relief. "You can come out now," he said, and opened the door and stepped out. "Welcome to my house."

'Well, I followed him into the sitting room and he

124

showed me how to get a cup of coffee by pressing a button. Au! That place was so full of gadgets you had to be a professor to know which button to push for what. In time, and I was there for sixteen years, I learnt how to operate most of the buttons in that house. Oh yes, it was just like a house, not a space ship, as you would imagine. It had a lounge, bedrooms, a kitchen, even a little toilet. The Ford was kept in the garage.

'In the basement was the Factory. Now, I didn't find out what was made there for many years. It was just where the Baas would go to work when he returned from his expeditions in the pickup.

'In the evenings, I would be made to get the dinner by pressing the right buttons in the kitchen. Then he would make me sit in the lounge with him and talk.

'He was always joking with me. He used to talk about visiting earth on different dates like you or me would talk of visiting, say, Brandfoort on one day and Potgietersrust on another. He would say, "I went to 1922 today, in summer. What a lovely weather you are having then!" and so on.

'One day I asked him what business he was in. "Farming, my boy, farming," and that was all he would say. I would have believed him if he had allowed me out of the house and there had been green fields outside. But all you could see through the windows was black, and big round lights far away. They did not look like stars as you and I know them. They were just lights, no twinkling or anything like that. There was no moon either.

'Well, as I grew older I became more and more curious about what was really going on. Besides, I was deadly bored by this solitary life and by the Baas's stories about 36 BC, or 1956, or 1785. Of course, he refused to talk about 1973, because that was when he was killed.

'One day when he was out in the truck, I decided to

explore the factory – which had been forbidden to me under the strongest threats.

'I went to the basement door, which was of course locked. I picked it open using the Swiss Army knife he had given me. Tiptoed down the stairs. The lights came on automatically, as they did in every room.

'There was every kind of machine there, au! And there was grease and dirt everywhere – you've never seen such dirt! Well, I had been trained to be a houseboy, so the first thing I did was run back upstair to get the broom and dustpan. Then I went downstair again and started to clean.

'When I got to a door marked *Store Room*, I went inside to clean that as well.

'This room was full of bits of people. There were skulls, fingers, an eye or two, stacks of sets of teeth. I couldn't believe what I was seeing. I ran out of there, and shut that door behind me. Then I raced up the stairs and tried to make the basement door look like no one had touched it.

'What was I to do? There were the scratch marks from the knife, the broken lock, all the evidence plain for the eye to see.

'So I sat in the lounge and decided to think. Think, brain! Who is this chap with the stripy skin? He is from another planet, that he had already told me. He could travel anywhere he liked. That he had also told me. Anywhere and *anywhen*, because he could travel through time as well.

'He said he was a farmer, and now I understood. He was a farmer of *people*! He was growing people for food. What had we been eating all this time?

'Well, there was only one thing to do. I would have to murder this murderer.

'There was no choice. There was no telephone, I could not call the police.

'You may laugh! But you know very well that the South African Police can go anywhere! There was only me to carry out the supreme sentence.

'I had planned it very carefully, or so I thought. He would be home soon. He would drive the pickup into the garage. There he would unload the corpses, and take them through into the basement. I don't know quite what he did then, but obviously the only time to get him would be as he got out of the truck and before he started to unload.

'So I went down to the garage with my Swiss Army knife and hid behind a pile of tyres, waiting for my master to come home.

'Finally, the door opened – and everything went black.

'I had forgotten that humans need oxygen to breathe, and while that door was open, all the oxygen was going out. It didn't bother him, of course, as he was in the truck.

'When I came round again, I was in my bedroom and he was sitting next to me waiting for me to recover.

' "So the sleeper awakes," he said. "Welcome back to the world!"

'When I saw him sitting there I was terrified. He must have found the broken-open door – and what about the knife in my hand?

' "Don't kill me, baas," I begged. "Please. I won't do it again."

' "Why should I kill you, you stupid boy? I can't do without you, you know that!"

' "But I—"

' "But you tried to kill me. Obviously. You were programmed to try to kill me. You were also programmed to be too stupid to succeed."

' "I don't understand—"

'So he explained to me everything. He told it like this: The Xichrans (the name is difficult to pronounce. If you say it right, it sounds like a cough) are farmers. They look for green planets where there are the beginnings of life. They then choose an appropriate animal

127

and inject it with a medicine called DeNa. This makes the animal develop intelligence and eventually dominate the planet. Then they are ready to be farmed.

'This DeNa dictates everything they do, so the Farmer knows what periods of their history it's best to visit for the best meat. Baas Karma told me that he usually preferred wars, though he steered clear of wars with A-bombs, because the meat was contaminated and unfit to eat. He also visited times when there were no wars, because sometimes he fancied fresh meat, rather than the staple diet of nineteen-year-old boys.

'Another reason was to subtly alter history if necessary to make sure that the right number of wars took place, or to alter society or civilisation for his own long-term needs. For example, he caused an increase in homosexuality when the world population was too high and brought back the Family when it was too low. Things like that.

'By the way, he told me that there have been four atomic wars on earth already. They are necessary when pollution gets too high, as this also contaminates the meat, so mankind has to start all over again.'

'Are you trying to tell me that this Baas Karma is what we call God?' Pieter asked, a little annoyed by what he saw as Umfaan's heresy.

'Wait. You will see.

'Anyway, another thing to remember, he could not visit earth after 1973, because that was when he was killed by a bus whilst chasing a pretty little English nurse called Susan.

'So he made me an offer. He had decided to go into export in a big way. Up to now he had been a subsistence farmer – that means he farmed just for his own needs. However, he was convinced that after 1973 there was a vast amount of good meat to be found. He had been working on the world very hard since 1967, trying to prevent the next atomic war, reduce pollution and cigarette smoking, improve health by right eating and exercise, and so on. And then to get so carelessly killed had annoyed him very much.

'So he had picked me up to train as his assistant. He had brought me up to know exactly how everything in the house worked, and now, if I was willing, he would show me how to drive the pickup so that I could visit Earth after 1973 to see how things had turned out and pick up large consignments for export.'

Pieter's home life altered radically between 1962 and 1966. This was largely due to the change in the status of the Mostert family when his father became Mayor of Ventersdaal. The transformation of the drunken reprobate into the foremost citizen of the town happened like this:

Japie, you will remember, had married Hester Strijdom, the ugly daughter of Jan Strijdom, the police chief. He had also fallen in love with her. This was not so hard to understand, for they were perfectly suited.

Hester, like Japie, enjoyed her drink and the lovebirds spent most of their evenings curled up round a bottle of KWV, listening to Springbok Radio and playing with various parts of each other, to the disgust of their children who invariably went to bed where Helena and Jakobus played with each other too, and Pieter was left to play with himself.

During the day when Japie was out in the fields, Hester would get bored. She had never been interested in being a mother, and she ignored the children most of the time. So Pieter spent much of his time with black people, while Helena and Jakobus played Doctors and Nurses.

Hester's life consisted of: Waking up before Japie at 5 a.m. and supervising the kitchen staff in preparing the breakfast. Then Japie and the kids would come to eat. After a mountain of steak and eggs had vanished down their throats, Japie would be off to the fields or the market, and the kids would be off to school.

Hester would then fuss around the house with Momsie the maid for a while pointing out dust here, unhoovered carpet there. Momsie would carry out her orders. Then there was nothing to do but have a little drinkie. Hester seldom went into the town, as she had no friends there. She didn't even do the shopping herself but gave a list to Kondisi, who did it for her.

Sometimes she fell asleep, and dreamt of being a princess in a fairy-tale world in which she was stunningly beautiful, and every knight was dying to marry her and every dragon dying to eat her.

Hester had, in fact, been a princess in ancient Wessex, England. She had been a great beauty, but had died in 874 AD in a fire in a barn, to which she had gone for a tryst with a knight called Sir Wylfred. Rumour at the time had it that a dragon called George had kidnapped her and taken her to the barn. The brave Sir Wylfred had dashed to her rescue, only to die with both princess and dragon in a great fire caused by George's carelessness with his incendiary breath.

This story (which had been invented by Wylfred's wife) was subsequently distorted into the Legend of St George and the Dragon.

In this life she was, in fact, a heavy-set woman with massive ham-hands, oily brown hair scraped back over her skull, a body like a barrel and legs like sewerage pipes.

But she was desperately romantic. Japie was her knight, who had rescued her from a miserable spinsterhood, and given her the unbelievable joys of sex for the first time in her life.

Her pregnancy and the subsequent birth of Pieter though had been a dreadfully sordid episode, an unwelcome interruption in her self-created wonderland. She preferred to forget it, and secretly ensured that it would never happen again by taking the Pill. Japie would have been furious if he had ever discovered this.

Despite her happiness at being married to Japie and his two thousand acres of excellent farmland, she was still waiting for her prince to come. After all, had not Genevieve, the wife of King Arnold, had a fling with a knight called Sir Lunchalot de Luck? (Her memories of the Tales of King Arthur were somewhat blurred by twenty years of excessive alcohol intake.)

One day her Prince came.

Hendrik De Jong was an elder of the church and the local Magistrate and a frequent visitor to the Mostert place. He had been a carousing buddy of Japie's during Japie's carousing days. They had a million hilarious stories to relive together. Hester had heard them all at least thirty-two times, and secretly resented the evenings when Hendrik came over and took her dear husband's attention away from her.

Then one night Hendrik brought his son Fanus along. Hester was surprised and thrilled. Strange that Hendrik never brought his pretty little wife Sarie to visit. She probably despised Hester. Perhaps, Hester thought, he wanted his son to hear the dreadful stories of Pa's wild youth, so that Fanus could see what a *man* Pappie was.

Fanus was the handsomest boy in the village, and probably the handsomest boy in the Transvaal. He was twenty years old and had gorgeous curly brown hair and irreverently blue eyes. His body was taut and strong, a Commando's body. He was a creature of steel, a weapon of war and though beautiful, his beauty was tinged with a thrilling hint of brutality.

As soon as Hester saw this paragon her knees trembled, her breath came in short gasps and she behaved as teenagers do when confronted by pure sex.

She sat opposite Fanus while his father and her husband rabbited on about the Good Ole Days, and her eyes interrogated the folds of his shirt which stretched itself over the rippling muscles, the denim trousers trying to restrain the arrogant bulge of his crotch.

131

Unrequited love is a charming obsession in youth. It is a tragedy when suffered by a forty-seven-year-old woman with a passing resemblance to a hippo.

As father and son left, Hester resolved that come hell or high water she would make the young man love her. And having discovered that Fanie was home on leave for the next few days, she resolved to visit him. So, one morning when the children were safely at school and her husband away to market, she dressed up in her best church dress, smeared deep red lipstick over her generous lips and lined her eyes smudgily with an eyebrow pencil. Then she got into her little Fiat and drove to Ventersdaal.

The de Jong house was in the middle of town. It was a fine two-storey Victorian building with a big garden, and it was decorated with an abundance of eccentric ironwork created by its original owner, who was an iron founder from Macclesfield in England.

Hester was greeted by a yappy little terrier at the front gate, whose ancestry could be traced back much further than hers. The dog said, 'Who the f*** hell is this c***? F*** off! *Voetsek!*' very loudly and persistently.

Impatient to get to her Prince, Hester gave the dog a savage kick which sent it yowling off into a bush with a couple of broken ribs, and went up to the front door.

She rang the bell. No answer. By now she was sweating heavily, desire and fear messing with her logic circuits.

There was no answer to her imperious ringing. Sarie was out clothes shopping. The servants were in their quarters sampling some especially good dagga from the Transkei.

She opened the unlocked door. No sign of anyone. Dammit, they must all be out somewhere.

She entered the living room. Strange. A shirt draped carelessly over the sofa. *His* shirt! A bound of heart, a catch of breath. Trembling, she picked it up and sniffed deeply around the armpits. Oh that man-smell, that mix of sweat and some strange perfume she had never smelled before.

Perfume?

The hippo was on heat. Nothing could have stopped her mounting the stairs to find his room, to see where he slept.

As she climbed the stairs she almost tripped over a pair of trousers. Oh ecstasy! *His* trousers. She smelled them too, maddened by the steamy odour of his crotch which clung like musk to the denim.

She steamed with desire. And the discovery of his underwear at the top of the stairs nearly brought her to orgasm, as she stroked them over her sweating body and face, leaving mad streaks of red and black.

Now, which was his door? *This* must be his door! A sock lay on the threshold. I will lie on the bed and sink in his smell and—

The tableau which nearly caused Hester a heart attack: The beautiful naked body of the young Commando all glistening with sweat and oil, lying atop the scrawny body of blond Freddie van Rensburg, the town hairdresser and notorious moffie.

'Argh!' Hester screamed.

'Argh!' the two men screamed in harmony.

'Argh!' Hester screamed again and bolted down the stairs. She collided, with a crunch, with Sarie who had just arrived home. Parcels littered the air. Then unable to bear reality any more, Hester fell into a deep faint on the living-room carpet.

She came round on the bed in the guest bedroom, to which she had been carried by the lovely Fanus. The first face she saw was his. Was the Sleeping Beauty being wakened by her Prince Charming? No. The hippo was being wakened by a moffie pervert.

'Are you all right now, Tannie?'

'Yes, I think so.' Then, remembering, 'You pervert!'

'Don't be like that, Tannie. It's not perverted to *me*.

Try to understand a little bit.'

'Let me handle this, Fanie,' said Sarie, who had been standing behind him. 'So now you know our little family secret, Mevrou Mostert. Our skeleton in the cupboard. Yes, I'm afraid Fanie was thrown out of the Commandos a year ago. He has been living in Johannesburg with a very nice young man—'

'A what! I think it's *disgusting*—'

'Some people do think that, but he *is* our son. This is the burden we have to bear—'

'It's no burden to *me*!' said Fanus, and swept out of the room.

Sarie sat on the chair by the bed. 'I suppose nothing I could do would persuade you not to tell anybody? Especially your father? Your husband? The scandal would break us.'

'Maybe not *nothing* . . .' said Hester. She may have been a romantic but she was also possessed of an animal cunning. Things were about to go her way. 'Let's talk of turkey,' she said.

They did. The result was a sudden and dramatic rise in the Mosterts' social status. Japie was invited to join the Broederbond. The Town Council voted him a place. In time, he became Mayor. The sponsorship of the De Jongs meant everything in the town.

And Hester never told anybody about the afternoon that changed their lives. As for her husband, he accepted his rise as the inevitable result of the First Law of the Dairy: Cream always rises to the Top.

Three

'And then what happened? Come on, Umfaan, finish your Science Fiction.'

'You can't tell the difference between fact and fiction *yet*? And I thought I had taught you so well.

Umfaan's History of the World
II The New Testament

'All right, so this is what happened: I accepted his offer. Maybe you think I was mad, but I had no choice. Also, I had my own plans.

'I stayed with him five more years, and he taught me everything he knew. He used to take me to all the "clean" wars, to load the pickup with bodies. He showed me how to process them in the factory and, most important, he showed me how to drive the pickup.

'After a while, I became the driver and he was content to be ferried from earth-time to earth-time.

'And then, when I knew everything, I killed him!'

Umfaan puffed his pipe and sat back with a grin.

'How did you do that, Umfaan?'

'Hah, simple! One day he wanted to visit 1857, the Indian Mutiny. I asked to stay at home, as there were still a few bodies left in the deep freeze, ready for processing, and I wanted it empty for his return.

'When he came back, he parked in the garage as usual. The door closed. He got out of the truck. From a control panel I had rigged up in the basement, I automatically locked the door from the basement into the garage. Then I opened the garage door. All the oxygen went out and he died. Then I closed the garage door, dragged his body to the trash disposal and ejected it out into space.'

'You mean—'

'Yes! That made me free to travel through all of space and time, to change history whenever I don't like it, and to rule the world! Ha ha ha hahahaha. Ha ha ha hahahaha.' He laughed, and laughed, for ages.

'That's a silly story, Pieter,' I said, as we sat together on the beach watching the remains of the sunset vanishing over the sea.

'Not so silly.'

'What do you mean?'

'Tom, I've *seen* the pickup.'

'You can't *believe* the story, can you? I mean, there are thousands of Ford pickups.'

'Don't be so sure. Anyway, every time I see a beaten-up old pickup with Witbank number-plates driven by an ancient black man, I get one helluva shiver down my spine.'

'You would.'

'Yes. Amazing sunset.'

'Yes.'

Yes, I met Pieter in Durban.

What an adventure Durban was for me. I booked into an incredibly seedy five-storey hotel called the Ocean View, even though the only ocean view available to its residents was to be had from the top of its roof. I had used another false name, Willie Peters. When I booked in I had enough money for two nights' accommodation, which, thankfully, included breakfast and dinner. What I would do after that was anybody's guess.

On my second day, I went strolling along the sea-front. And behold. Strolling aimlessly toward me came two lithe-legged visions in miniskirts. Joanna! Celeste!

'Tom!' Run, hug, kiss, breathless 'Whathaveyou, Wherehaveyou, Didyous' exchanged, we sat on a bench and told our thrilling stories.

'You vanished!' Joanna said. 'One day you were there, the next – your mother said she had no idea where you were.'

'That's true. She has no idea.'

'But why? What happened?'

'I ran away.' And I told her the story.

'Gosh,' she said. 'So did I!'

'How?'

'Well, I asked Daddy if Celeste and I could go on holiday together, since after all I'd finished exams and everything. He refused, completely and adamantly refused. ''Two little girls on their own,'' he said. Little girls! I ask you . . .'

Celeste laughed and slapped Joanna playfully on a knee. 'My parents said I could go,' she said triumphantly. 'Actually, I don't think they give a damn as long as I'm out of their way.'

'Where are you staying? Have you got any money?'

'Not a lot,' said Joanna and added after a rueful pout, 'At the Majestic.'

'That's posh,' I said.

'I've got a bit,' said Celeste. Her French parents were outrageously wealthy, much divorced and genuinely didn't give a damn about their daughter. Celeste by the way was thin, dark, very tall – madly sexy. Her face was boyish, high cheekbones and short hair. She gave the impression of having Serious Muscles under her loose cotton blouse.

'What are we going to do for money?' I asked. 'I've got a survival problem here. I'm on my last—'

'We've – got a scheme,' said Joanna. She exchanged a should-I-tell-him look with Celeste, who nodded. 'But look, this is *very* secret, OK?'

'Sure. Consider me a Closed Box. Drop your secret in.'

137

Joanna glanced around to make sure no one was listening. 'We're – how do I put this – um, whoring.'

'Huh?'

'Whoring. Selling our bodies. Well, we haven't had a trick yet—'

'Trick?'

'That means client, darling. It's the jargon we use.'

'Oh!' My 'Oh' is a deep groan from the heart. It means, Oh shit, here I am, been trying to get into your pants for a *year* fa chrissake, and you're talking about *selling* it— 'Well. Fine. That's great.'

'You don't sound very pleased. Don't tell me you've gone *moral* since I saw you last.'

'Well, no, no! Of *course* not!'

'Why don't you come in with us—' Celeste asked.

'I'm not pretty enough.'

'Don't be silly. I've got a really bright idea. Listen to this.'

So that's what happened. We would go into a bar, and the two girls would sit at a table while I roamed about the place. I would seek out a randy, rich-looking potential, wait until he started eyeing up my two friends, then go up to him and explain that he could have their favours for a small consideration, paid to me. He could pick one, or, if he were so inclined, both.

It worked perfectly, even on the first night. We made forty rand that evening, and ten of it was for me.

On the next night we made a hundred. Off one trick. They 'liberated' his wallet. I was terrified. But Joanna explained that there was no way the fellow would go to the police, and say that he had been robbed by two whores.

The nice kids from the Northern Suburbs had discovered crime.

We moved to a better hotel on the seafront. I had a room on the first floor and they occupied a suite above me. The arrangement was excellent. The nights were thrilling.

Durban is a busy port on the one hand, and a thriving seaside resort on the other. The two worlds are kept absolutely apart. The smart holidaymakers didn't know the scummy harbour existed, except as a possible sightseeing spot. The sailors, dockers, etc., did know that there was an elegant world lining the seafront at the end of West Street, but they would no more consider going there than Howard Hughes would have considered visiting a leper colony.

The city was speckled with every kind of night club you could imagine, from the ultra-swish, through Bohemian jazz, to the sailors' places where booze, blood and sex were commoner than cockroaches. Which, incidentally, were everywhere.

The people of the city are mostly Indian. They have a massive grimy market where the tourists buy anything from saris to DP. DP is a very special kind of dagga. They take the fresh young heads of the marijuana plant and roll them into a tight stick of brown paper. The secret – and this is *very* secret, hear? – is the addition of a drop of saturated sugar solution to the grass before it's rolled. This causes fermentation, and makes the smoke absolute dynamite.

No, you don't smoke the brown paper stick. You open it and crush the stuff into a little tobacco, roll the mixture up in a cigarette paper. *Then* you smoke it.

One of my visits to Tuxedo Junction, a jazz club in the port, resulted in my breathless discovery of 'tabs'. These were dexamphetamine or speed. They fuelled endless sleepless days and nights of frantic rushing from bar to club to beach, talking talking dry-mouthed to speeding contemporaries. Joanna and Celeste loved them too. Tabs enabled them to increase our turnover to a ridiculous level.

One night I went to their suite early, to pick them up for the night's business. I arrived at their door at the same time as two evil-looking men in suits.

'What do you want?'

139

'Piss off, pimp,' one said, bashing me out of the way. 'These whores got my money. I want it back.' He reached for the door handle.

Fuelled by speed, I threw myself at him. He was unprepared for my fury. My arms whirred like a mad propeller. His pal lurched at me. A knife appeared. I don't know how I did it, but I snatched at the knife, cutting my hand open. He let go. I grabbed it. Slashed him across the chest . . .

Then they ran away. I leaned against the door half fainting, amazed by my efficiency at the art of violence, sick at the thought of having hurt someone.

The dexedrine was running low. I began to weep.

Then I opened the door, and the girls were entangled on the bed together, faces buried in each other's wet parts, and I couldn't have been more shattered if you had slapped me across the face with a wet whale.

They looked up and saw me there with the knife in one blood-dripping hand and they froze in mid-ecstasy. 'Tom!' 'Tom, come here!' but I left.

I went down to my room and washed the cut and wrapped it with toilet paper. Then I poured twenty dexedrine out into my good hand and dropped them down my throat, no water.

I wrapped the knife in toilet paper too and put it in my inside pocket, and went out, into the Durban sunset.

A long sunset beach. A knife thrown out as far as it will fly. A boy mad with speed hustling swish-swish down the sand. A hank of bloodied toilet paper trailing raggedly from one hand. He is talking wildly to himself. He is discussing his life, like with St Peter.

'And how did you spend your time on earth—Oh, I think I may have killed somebody but apart from that—Didn't I hear that you were a pimp—Oh I might have been but that just happened, I mean, I never

140

planned to be a pimp—And is it true you take drugs and are a notorious raver—Oh I do rave a bit but nearer my God to Thee—And hast thou not beaten up thy father and given thy mother much aggravation—That may be true but I do have a good heart and—And hast thou not lied to a very nice man who is a Headmaster at one of My schools, who did nothing but good by you—I might have done but what can one do when one is on the run dum de dum' (Starts singing) 'Oh what have I done tum-te-tum I killed a man on the run-de-dum, given my papa not a lot of fun ho hum, doo-be-doo-be—Be serious—I can't – Oh shit I can't go back to the hotel ever. If they catch me – did that guy die?' (Sings again) 'My my, did the guy die, I don't know why-y-y, oh my oh my . . .'

Miles from Durban he sits on a bit of beach and the infernal eternal internal monologue carries on and on.

'Hi.'

'What?'

'Môre. Wat maak jy hier?'

I try to stand but suddenly I feel sick and have to sit down again, head swimming. A gawky, gangling, blond young man reaches down concernedly, stops me falling back. Police? No, too awkward, too helpful. Typical farm boy. In cut-down denim shorts, crazily coloured Hawaiian shirt, much too big.

'Is jy siek?' he peers into my face, his own washed with concern. Usual reaction to an Afrikaner is instant antipathy. But no defences left and there's so much warmth in his farm-boy face and God I need warmth; I nearly melt entirely.

'Please sit with me for a while.'

'You are English?' It's funny how I expect everybody – black, Afrikaans – to speak English with me. I refused then to speak Afrikaans even though, like all South Africans, I am bilingual.

Obviously. 'Obviously.'

'Are you sick?' He sits next to me.

141

'No, I'm fine. I just need somebody to talk to.'

'What happened to your hand?'

'I um – was attacked.'

'By who?'

'Oh, no one. Well – tell me about you. Who are you? What are you doing in Durban?'

'My name is Pieter Mostert. I'm from a little town in the Eastern Transvaal called Ventersdaal. As to what I am doing here . . .'

Pieter told me.

He had just received the results of his Matriculation exam, and busting with amazement at the predominance of As and Bs had roared off to the town in his mother's Fiat to celebrate with a bunch of his buddies.

Things I have not told you about Pieter: First, he was a fanatical rugby player, a common idiosyncrasy amongst small-town Afrikaans boys, who all dream of becoming a Springbok one day and beating the shit out of the Lions, or All Blacks – which isn't likely to happen as none of those teams would play against South Africa. He was even Captain of the school team. The bunch of buddies with whom he celebrated his success in the exams were all rugby-team boys.

The second thing I haven't mentioned, though you might well have guessed: Pieter had a slightly different view of Blacks to that of his contemporaries. Which was strange, considering that his father was Mayor, he was Captain of the rugby team and he had done rather well at school, all of which made him the perfect Afrikaner, beloved of dominees, town dignitaries, anybody who was – if you'll excuse the phrase – anybody. A great future was planned for the boy: he would end up, everybody predicted, as a politician and leading light in the Nationalist Party. Or, at the very least, an important figure in the Dutch Reformed Church.

Yes, but becoming those things required an unquestioning obedience to the holy tenets of Apartheid.

Which is jolly difficult when one has discovered that Blacks are people, too.

OK, back to that evening when Pieter grabbed Mammie's car and drove to the Station Hotel in Ventersdaal to celebrate the end of his school career, and his success.

They were all waiting for him. Frikkie, Hennie, Loadie, Kobus, Jannie, Ivan, Dawid, twelve of them (I don't remember the other names – more of the same I suppose), good Afrikaners and true, full of muscle and animal energy, awkward overgrown creatures with voices incapable of speaking below 13 decibels, laughs which could make the feathers on a rooster stand on end. The products of years of indoctrination, as unable to question the values of their fathers as a dead chicken is to cross the road.

The party began at 7.30. They were expelled from the bar three hours later having done irreparable damage to the vast slab of marble which had supported many a drunkard since 1897, when it had made the perilous sea voyage from Carrara in Italy, just to be in Ventersdaal in time to be smashed by a bunch of drunken schoolboys.

Pieter was as much to blame as anybody. He had joined in everything, as was expected from the team captain.

So they found themselves standing, leaning, swaying outside the Station Hotel at eleven in the evening with a furious hotel manager yelling invective and promising to make all their parents pay, and they had nowhere to go and were still wild and wanted to party.

Which one suggested going to the Pandokkies? If it was Pieter, he didn't admit it to me. 'There's a shebeen there. We can drink till morning.' Somebody must have said that.

They piled into two cars, Pieter's mum's and Dawie's daddy's 1957 Chevrolet. This was a monster-sized machine with tail fins, powder blue and Dawie's dad's pride. He had lent it to his son with many dire warnings.

Whooping, yelling, the carloads of rugby club zig-zagged through the going-to-bed town. Heads popped out of windows, cursed or laughed according to the views of their owners, then popped back in again. One belonged to the Chief of Police who, recognising the driver of one of the cars as his grandson, gave a deep chortle and climbed back into his lustless bed.

Boys will be boys.

On the way to the hill road one of the cars knocked over an old black man on a bicycle. He later died of exposure because no one noticed him lying in the ditch for three days. Here we go again.

Boys will be boys.

They had to park the cars at the bottom of the path, and, singing a filthy rugby song they staggered arm in arm up the hill to the Pandokkies.

Selina came out of her shack, hands on hips, a gargantuan obstacle. '*Hé*, what's all this? What animals are here?'

'Selina,' Piet shouted, 'it's me, Pieter. Hallo, my darling!' and ran up to her and kissed her. The others laughed, because they thought Pieter's greeting was a mocking one, they didn't know how much he loved this vast old blackwoman.

'What's all this trash you've brought along?' Selina pushed him off, eyeing his companions belligerently.

'These are my *friends*, Selina. We only want a little drink, Selina, maybe some dancing?' He tried a wobbly waltz and nearly fell down. 'And maybe some girls? And maybe some dagga? We've *all* passed, Selina. Well, all except Jannie but what do you expect from a half-back—' Roars of laughter which could probably be heard for miles.

'There's *too* many people here, Pieter. Are you *mad* to bring these boys here? You'll get me in trouble.'

144

'Come on, kaffir.' Dawid Pretorius is the biggest and ugliest of the team. His ears are squashed. His face is round. He is known as 'Animal'. His body looks fat but it's all muscle. Especially between the ears. 'Give us the booze. Don't make trouble.'

Uh oh. Pieter's boozy euphoria clears a bit. Feels like trouble about to – 'Take it easy, Animal,' he mutters.

'Come on, where's the booze?' Frikkie yells.

'You do what you're told, kaffir,' Jannie adds. The team joins in.

Pieter is starting to have the same feeling as the father who has given his baby a hand-grenade to play with.

Behind Selina Pieter sees a bunch of dark shadows emerging from the darker shadows of the huts. Tattered black men, labourers on the local farms, each carrying a weapon of some sort – picks, knobkerries, sjamboks.

Oh shit.

'Come on, chaps, let's get out—'

Animal jumps into the air with a bloodlusty howl. At last! Action! 'Get them, boys!'

THE BATTLE OF THE PANDOKKIES

At the approach of the invaders the women and children from the little cluster of huts left, to hide amongst the rocks and bushes a little way above the battleground on the side of the hill. Except, of course, Selina, the unofficial Queen of the Pandokkies.

They had long been expecting a visit from the police, and had prepared for invasion. So the arrival of the pack of rugby hooligans had sent every able-bodied man into the corner of the hut where he had hidden his weapon, while the Queen went out to parley with the invaders.

Her failure, followed by the attack.

Into the battle stormed the twelve – drunk, unarmed, fighting mad. Thud of flesh on flesh. Shouts of Here! Here! Au! Kobus, get him off! Here, Jannie, he's yours! Get the kaffirs!

Most of the battle took place amidst the huts. Eventually the stove in Selina's shack was knocked over. Fire. Fire! Hennie grabbed a burning brand and ran from hut to hut making the fire breed. More fire! Men with burning shirts, mad with fury.

Rocking, roaring with laughter, retreat of the triumphant rugby team, leaving behind a furiously burning group of shacks with black men running here and there with water, trying to rescue bits of furniture, clothes, their possessions turning into carbon and smoke.

'Kom, Pietie. Waai huis toe!'

But Pieter was standing by, hugging a weeping, screaming Selina, Boadicea cheated of her rightful place at the head of her people by the restraining arms of her adoptive traitor-son. 'Go! Get away,' Pieter yelled. 'You idiots, go away!'

Dawid swaggers up to Pieter. 'Are you coming with us or not? Come on.'

'Go!' Selina screams at him. 'Look what you have done. Go with your *boere* friends! Go!'

'No, I'm staying.'

'Kaffir-boetie! Kaffir-lover!' says Dawid, and the others take up the taunt. 'Kaffir-lover!' and then, clinging to all parts of the Chevrolet, they drive off, a triumphal procession, to tell everybody about the Defeat of the Kaffirs. Oh what a grand night.

Boys will be boys.

Leaving Pieter being yelled at by a maddened Selina. 'What have you done? Look! Look at my house. Was I good to you? Was I always good to you? I brought you up. I gave you food. I loved you like my son.'

Pieter, stone cold sober, wants her to hit him but she won't let him off that lightly.

146

'Go away. Leave me here. Go away.'

She sat on the stony earth. 'Go away. Leave here.'

He stared numbly, then head drooping between his shoulders shuffled to the car and drove home, crying.

Where was Umfaan in all this? I don't know.

The next day Pieter announced to his parents that he would be going to Durban on holiday. He was going alone, and he was taking the car. He didn't ask permission. He stated his intentions. Neither mother nor father bothered to argue. Their son had grown up, all of a sudden. They were proud. They gave him money and helped him pack.

'And you? What's your story?'

I tell him. Everything, from the fight with my father to the recent events in Durban. He is fascinated. I don't know why I'm telling him everything. Possibly because he drinks it all in like a plant that has been stuck, gasping, in a desert for far too long.

His attention is delicious. I offer him a handful of tabs. To my surprise he accepts and so began three wild days of frantic raving. In so many ways we were alike. We were like lovers in those days in everything but sex, twined about each other's psyches, sleeplessly exchanging our lives and finding pure pleasure in each other.

In his car, in his hotel room, in clubs, on the beach.

Then the pills ran out. The Grand Comedown. Brains drying up. Deep sighs of chemically induced depression and loss which could only be salved by more tabs.

My money, clothes and pills were in that hotel room, the Scene of the Crime. We discussed how to get these things endlessly.

Unable to resist any longer, bugger the consequences, I went back to the hotel. Pieter waited around the corner while I, sick with comedown, pill-thin and unshaven, went shaking into the lobby and asked for my key.

147

It was given without question. Whew! Then the Indian desk clerk said, 'I think this is for you.' He handed me a telegram. The envelope was marked 'Willie Peters a.k.a. Tom Bloch'. Gasp of terror. Were the police arresting me by telegram? Silly.

Rush up to the room. Eat tabs. Shaking, I opened the envelope.

'Tom darling stop,' it read. 'We will be at Umhlanga Rocks from the fifteenth stop we hope you will join us there stop Love Mom.'

What. Gosh. How. Oh hell, it's the fifteenth today. I pack; already the pills are working their remarkable pickup. One last thing to do.

Rush up one flight of stairs and knock timidly on the girls' door.

It is answered by a fat woman in curlers. 'Sorry, wrong room.' Downstairs again, pick up my case and dash down to the lobby. There I find it impossible to slip past the desk, so I pay and rush out to Pieter.

Grab him, force him to do a self-conscious waltz. 'Pieter, I'm not a murderer! Or if I am, no one knows! Everything's all right. Look!'

Four

So I was restored to the heaving, scented bosom of my family in the lush surroundings of the Umhlanga Rocks Hotel where we were served with oysters, lobsters, steaks, an interleading suite, grovelling staff, palm trees and aspidistras. Plowsky and Michelle were a little distant with me. But Mother was tearfully delighted at the reunion. Strange, but Father treated me with friendliness, and I suppose, even respect. He actually spoke to me as an equal. Amazing.

148

What I didn't realise then was, Daniel had been very impressed by all the money I seemed to have. That's my boy. Don't know how he got it but.

Most nights, after the fam had gone to bed, there would be a tap at my French doors which opened on to the beach. I would let Pieter in and we would eat pills and smoke DP. Sometimes we went on endless walks along the night beach. Or we'd get into his car and drive to Durban and rave away in clubs till morning. Or we'd just talk all night.

By breakfast I would be wide-eyed and ragged, but the parents never commented. I slept by the swimming pool most of the day. I wonder what they thought.

They had found me, by the way, with the aid of a Private Detective, Joey Morgan. He must have been pretty good.

One

On my return, there was just one letter waiting for me. 'Official. Amptelik.' My Army call-up papers.

Oh bloody swear. I had forgotten the Army.

The medical passed (why the hell did my bloody parents pay some idiot all those years ago to put things in my shoes to correct my flat feet?), a train ride to Tempe, a training camp stuck in a desert in the middle of the Orange Free State.

Oh the tearful farewell. For Anne, anyway. Waving handkerchiefs. Scene from an American war movie. Off to the Front.

THE ARMY

In 1966, every fit young White had to give nine months of his life to his country. It's two years these days, I believe. They need a lot more defence now.

There were three levels in camp hierarchy amongst

the conscripts: *Roofie* (literally, 'scab') for the first three months; *Blougat* ('Bluebum') for the next three, and *Ouman* for the last ('old man', of course).

Basic Training: 'Call this *square*, roofie?' (pointing to the blanket on the bed). 'See that tree. Are you back yet, roofie?' 'Clean it again – there's a speck.' (The rifle.) 'You dropped your rifle, roofie! Now fuck it.' 'Short arm inspection! Get your cocks out and stand by the bed!' 'Make these boots shine like a mirror. Piss on it and rub!' Are my puttees white enough does my brass reflect the sun can I see my face in my boots. Is this shirt ironed stiff does the collar cut my throat. Are my shorts long enough. Is my hair too long.

March march. Shoot shoot. Drill drill.

Get up. Five o'clock already. Cold shower, shivering naked bodies totally sexless.

I got fit for the first time in my life. It felt OK. There were no drugs to be had during Basic, the first three months. But I survived. Some people weren't so lucky.

I watched the Army break the vulnerable ginger-haired Wallace Meredith. He split open and runny green stuff ran out and so did he.

One day, Pieter walked into the barracks. Gosh, wild embrace, much catching up. It was a Sunday, and the Christians were on church parade. 'Why aren't you in church?'

'I told them I'm Muslim.'

'Idiot!'

'Let's go for a smoke—'

'What! You've got something with you?'

'Of course.' So we went off to the toilets where we sat on our individual crappers and passed the joint under the wall. Riddled with giggles, we went back to the barracks.

From then on, the Army became more OK.

In fact, I hated leave. I'd ache to get back to Pieter,

and a world where everything was predictable, and the only excitement was in learning how to screw the system.

The greatest challenge was Avoiding Route Marches. This required terrific timing, and courage.

'Platoon, quick – MARCH!' and just as the platoon on its way to join the battalion passed the toilets – slip out of line, *zap*! And into the bog at exactly the same time as the sergeant turned to lead the platoon.

Reunion in the bog.

One time, we decided to find somewhere to have a quiet smoke and wandered off to the target range. There was a chicken-wire enclosure next to the line of targets. We lay out there in the sun, among the spare targets, smoking, talking, giggling. Suddenly a volley of shots. Shit! The troops were peppering the targets right next to us.

Oh dear, well, if we keep perfectly still we're probably safe. Unless someone turns out to be a lousy shot. Well, if we creep into the enclosure we'll be safer . . .

Whizzz, pop! Pardon? Whizzz, pop! Small metal canisters come bounding into our little haven. Gas. Tear gas. Clouds of smoke. Cough hack weep. Bastards practising for the Revolution on our patch.

Giggling, weeping, we fight our way through the smoke and find ourselves in the middle of our platoon, returning from the route march.

Lucky thing, that.

We weren't a very popular pair amongst the psychopaths who were our NCOs. Strutting little tyrants with muscular arses and swagger-sticks. Them, not me, though I think I gave a passable impression of being a soldier. I did all the things they wanted me to do.

One of the things Pieter and I talked about endlessly was politics. I was the first 'white liberal' Pieter had ever met, and it was a revelation to him. He was surprised that even though I was against the system, I wasn't a Communist. But then, of course, I would have had horns and vampire teeth. He was also surprised to discover that he agreed with most of what I said. He had an inquiring and original mind.

This was his secret: He wanted to be one of the Thirty-Six Just Men Umfaan had told him about. He applied his considerable intellect to every question, with a massive attempt, in each case, to be totally objective.

What would the Just Man decide?

That the political system in South Africa could not be described as Just.

I am full of admiration for Afrikaners who have the courage to be objective about the plight of their 'nation'.

One day Pieter and I had an opportunity to put our beliefs to the test.

Two

Absolom Molapo had been in prison for five years. Like political prisoners all over the world, his life was circumscribed by little questions, and Great Ones.

The little questions: Will I be alone today or will that Bloemsma come for a 'chat'. Will he bring the whip this time. Will I get a cigarette from Abrahams. Will I be allowed a visit. Will the lawyer come. Can I get away with this sentence in this letter. Will the letter get to its destination at all. Will they transfer me to a better jail.

The Great Questions: Should I have joined the PAC or will the ANC triumph. Will the Revolution release me or must I wait on so-called White Justice. What is happening outside.

The only relief Absolom had from these thoughts was

when he was allowed out to work in the fields. This gave him a precious opportunity to talk to other prisoners, albeit with great circumspection. Occasionally he learnt things.

His apparent 'betrayal' of Muna had resulted in his being allowed a few limited privileges. To tell the truth, his captors had decided that he was no longer dangerous. They believed that if they let him out, the ANC wouldn't let him walk the streets unmolested – they would want revenge.

Absolom played on this.

His interrogator was a bull-faced Major called Jan Bloemsma. This animal was deeply offended by the fact that the Blacks weren't grateful for their little homelands. He couldn't understand why so many people wasted so much time trying to undermine the Government.

He had the intelligence of a rat in a maze – it was all he knew. He had worked out all the routes. It was right and proper. So he took a sadistic delight in keeping Absolom apparently terrified by the prospect of release.

The relationship between these two men was based on hatred for each other's politics. They hated what the other stood for, the cardboard cut-out image. Yet during the four years they had spent in their roles of prisoner and interrogator, they had developed a mutual respect and liking for the person buried within the role.

Absolom liked Bloemsma's dogmatism and inherent honesty. Bloemsma was farming stock, tied to earth. He liked dogs. So did Hitler. He was a dedicated father. So was Papa Doc.

Bloemsma was surprised and intrigued by Absolom's articulacy. He, like most white South Africans, was used to Blacks who wouldn't look him in the eye, and who did what they were told. Absolom was an intellectual challenge, and he saw their discussions as a test of the superiority of the white man.

He was continually trying to score points. A crazy

game of one-upmanship which Absolom was forced to play.

'Hallo, Molapo. Did you sleep last night?'

'They're leaving the light on all night again.'

'Are they?' (Clucks with hidden smile.) 'I'll see what I can do about thet. May I sit down?' He sits on the single chair. 'You have been reading the Bible!'

'There's nothing else to read. Have you considered my application for some books?'

'Considered, yes. But we have to check all those books. Make sure none of them is Communist propaganda, or immoral.'

'Alice in Wonderland?'

'You didn't ask for that, did you?'

'Yes. And *War and Peace.*'

'Aha! That's Russian.'

'Pre-revolutionary.'

'So you think South Africa is pre-revolutionary?'

'I didn't say that. But of course it is.'

'You Blacks live on false hopes. The South African Army is the most powerful in Africa. You haven't got a hope.'

'And you Whites are fooling yourselves if you think the people can be kept under by force of arms.'

'I don't understand you! You Communists spend all your time agitating to make a revolution, when even your own people just want a peaceful life; they are happy as they are.'

'We always have the same discussion. I prove you wrong every time but you just repeat the same arguments the next time. I'm tired of it.'

'Is that why you betrayed your colleagues?'

'What do you mean?'

'You begin to see that we are right, that there is no hope for your revolution?'

Absolom changed the subject. 'How's your spy? Muna the rat?'

'He was hanged. We pinned the station bomb on

156

him.' Bloemsma laughs. 'He wasn't any use to us any more. Your pals knew it was him who gave us the goods on you. Besides, he confessed to the bomb.'

'What did you do to him to make him confess?'

'Don't push too hard, Molapo. The guilty always confess. The innocent have nothing to say. We've got *justice* here.'

'You have. You've got Justice for the Whites and Laws for the Blacks.'

'It's the same thing.'

'No it's not.'

'You and me have to get to business, Molapo. There are still names to be told. I want details. Now tell me about that meeting in 1960, the one we were talking about yesterday. Who was it who said that violence is the only way?'

'I don't remember.'

'Look we know each other too well. Be reasonable. You are ours now. Your fate is in our hands. If we let you go they'll cut your balls off. You might as well empty yourself, give us everything you know.'

'I have already. What more—'

'Sometimes I just don't understand you, Molapo. You seem intelligent, but you say some bloody stupid things. If you don't tell us everything, you know very well that we will have to—'

'Don't make all those boring threats again. We both know you won't let me go unless you want me killed. And I'm too useful for you to kill me in here like you did all those others.'

'That's not the point. And don't you say I'm boring, Molapo, I don't like that. No, I mean that much as I would hate to have to do it, when my superiors insist on more information, I'll have to let Van Jaarsveld loose on you again.'

Van Jaarsveld was the sjambok man. He could use the whip like Grapelli can use the violin.

Absolom was in a classic Catch-22 situation. He

knew that the only way he could gain his freedom would be to betray, and betray again. If they did let him go, he would be expected to work for them. And they would watch his every move.

None of the information he had given so far was really new to them. Even so, they seemed to believe that he was co-operating to some extent. And they had let the news of this leak out.

Which made life outside the safe confines of the prison somewhat dangerous for Absolom.

So, year after year, the game went on. It was making Bloemsma prematurely grey. He knew that unless he really got the goods out of Molapo, he would never get promotion, never be released from a role which gave him no long-term satisfaction, even though it did provide odd, predictable pleasures.

Had it not been for Fate and Tom Bloch, the game would have lasted for ever. The two combatants would have grown old together, sitting in that cell, or in the interrogation room, reliving their arguments, repeating their theme songs year after year. Perhaps they would smoke their pipes together and grow to resemble two old friends with decades of shared experiences, chatting away at sunset.

Three

Pieter and I discovered an excellent way to enjoy route marches. There was this cough mixture, see, which, if you were to be crazy enough to drink a whole bottle, resulted in the most amazing hallucinations. Not the sort of hallucinations you get on, say, acid where what there *is* starts to flow about all over the place and bend and twist and turn into flowers and jewels and things. The Mixture's hallucinations came out of nowhere and had no relation to anything except the deepest bits of the mind.

Like, a wall would suddenly have portholes out of which poured snakes. An ashtray would suddenly be full of razorblades. That kind of thing.

We didn't regard the hallucinations as frightening at all. They were just movies, more fun, less predictable than anything Hollywood could manage. Being able to see them this way was a jolly good trick – a function of the Overmind, otherwise known as the Nevermind, which Umfaan taught me, through Pieter, through a story he told my friend a long time ago.

The Harvest of the Nevermind

'The first time I ever saw a battle was in 79 AD at a place called Masada, in a little Roman colony called Judea. You know the place? They call it Israel now. Silly name.

'Baas Karma had driven me there in the hope of rich pickings, and to show me how the harvesting operation works, and so on.

'When we arrived there, we had to park the pickup out of sight of the Jews, who were on top of this great hill defending the fortress, which was surrounded by Romans. There had not been a great deal of killing yet as the siege had just started, so there wasn't much to do except observe. So we made a little campfire and waited for the work to begin.

'After a few days we were getting very bored, so we captured a couple of Roman soldiers who had snuck off to have sex in the wood, and stole their uniforms. Then we ate them.

'Now we could go into the Roman camp and find out what was causing this tiresome delay. We had a schedule to keep!

'We were greeted by a centurion who had probably never before seen a Roman soldier with red- and green-striped skin and another who was black all over. "*Ave*," he said. He was puzzled. *Very* puzzled. "*Maria*," I answered, remembering the Catholic ritual. The Baas clapped me on the head and explained to the Centurion that I was an idiot. In Latin, of course.

'He later translated their discussion for me, which went like this:

' "Where are you from, soldier?"

' "From Britain, Centurion. We are conscripts."

' "Ah, that's why you paint your skin! Well, we do things differently here."

' "But we are keen for battle, Centurion."

' "So am I, soldier. So am I."

' "Then, why are we waiting? Why do we not attack?"

' "Have you not seen how well defended they are, Briton?"

' "Yes, Centurion."

' "Well, why waste men in an attack when we can sit here and starve them out."

' "Oh shit. I hadn't thought of that."

' "That's why we Romans beat you British. *You* don't think."

'The Baas grabbed me by the arm and pulled me away. He was furious. "Oh bugger, blast it!" he said. "Those bastards are going to starve them to death. There'll be nothing worth harvesting when it's all over! Damn damn damn! We'll have to resort to the Archangel ploy."

' "What's that, baas?"

' "Come with me." So we went back to the Ford, and started to do it up. We painted the wheels with gold paint. We stuck cottonwool to the back, to look like clouds. We cut out great big pieces of cardboard to look like wings, and stuck them to either side. Then we put firecrackers in strategic places, with long fuses we could activate from the cab.

'By the time night came, we were almost finished, and it was time to dress ourselves. So we cut up a couple of sheets and stuck silver-foil wings to our backs.

'When I saw him in this gear I started to shriek with laughter. We looked like a couple of angels from a Nativity play. "The only thing missing, baas, is the haloes!" "Hah!" he said, all serious, "you have a lot to learn. They haven't even invented haloes yet. So pay attention and do what I say!"

' "OK." So we got into the truck and took off, and very quickly we were circling above the fortress where about four hundred men, women, children witnessed our arrival with great shouts of joy and much religious activity. We set off the fireworks as we hovered above, and they all dropped to their knees and waved their arms in the air.

'Goodness, I thought. What a pleasure to be treated as an angel for a change!

'Well, we landed there in the middle of the fort, and they all crowded round the pickup. Then one grey hair with ages of beard came up to us. "It took you long enough," he said in ancient Hebrew. "I know you've been busy Great One, but we need you right now."

' "Hi, Jess," said Karma. "Sorry to keep you waiting but." He introduced me to the greybeard who was apparently an old friend. "This is Jess Korsten, origin-ally a countryman of yours. Jess, meet Umfaan, my apprentice."

' "Hi," I said.

' "Yes, Jess did a little job for me a coupla years back, right Jess?" They spoke now in Afrikaans so the others wouldn't cotton on.

' "Little job, he calls it! I had to hang on this stupid tree for ages by a couple of two-inch nails before he cut me down."

' "And are you beginning to see *why*?" Karma asked.

' "Not really, to be honest. But what about all this little lot now? You told them they were the Chosen People. Frankly, they're a little upset about starving to death."

' "Um, yes I can see that. But there is an alternative."

' "What's that?"

' "Well, how about killing each other?"

' "What?"

' "What?"

'The second unbelieving "What" was from me. Well, I knew Baas Karma had a job to do but usually the meat was ready killed before export.

'I looked around and there were all these women and children armed to the teeth, and their men looking every bit like heroes, and they seemed a nice bunch of people.

' "You can't *do* this, baas," I said, as a cute little kid with cow-brown eyes clung to my sheet, looking up at me with adoration.

' "Shut up, Umfaan," said Karma. "If you go soppy on me, I'll— you'll join them!"

' "Are you sure about this, God old pal?" asked Jess.

' "Of course I'm sure. Do you want to see this lot starve before your eyes? If you think those Roman buggers are going to go away, you can forget it! You've annoyed them too much for that."

' "Right as usual, old chap," said Jess. "Well, are you going to make the announcement or shall I?"

' "Oh I'll do it. It'll carry more authority. Right, you lot," he said in Hebrew, addressing the crowd. "I bring you good news!"

'Babble of "What?", "What news?", et cetera.

' "Because you have all served me so well and killed lots of Romans in the past, I have decided that you can all come to Heaven with me. Right now."

' "Gosh", "Great", "When do we start?" and so on.

' "Come on, I don't have all day! Those who don't

162

want to kill themselves can get someone else to kill them."

'Well, you've never seen anything so awesome as all that blood, as everybody killed everybody else while Baas Karma stood there and watched, with Jess standing at his side. I bowed my head and wept because I was very very upset.

'When they had finished, Karma turned to Jess. "Well?" he asked.

' "Well, I'm glad everything has gone so well. I'll be off then."

' "Wait," Karma commanded, and handed him a sword. "They'll need you along!"

' "Oh blast," the old prophet said, and stabbed himself to death.

' "Come on, Umfaan," said Karma. "Let's get loaded up."

' "No," I said, folding my arms.

' "Umfaan, I said *load up*. What's the matter with you?"

' "I can't believe you made all that happen. Did you see that little kid? How could you *do* that, just so we could fill our quota?"

' "Don't be an *ass*, Umfaan. That kid wouldn't have been cute after a couple of weeks without any food. What's the *sense* in them starving to death?"

' "But—"

' "Never mind but. And did I lie to them? I told them they would be going to Heaven, and they will."

' "That's true but—"

' "So load up!"

'Well, I did, Pietie, but all the time I was thinking, OK, fine, that's the way you like to do it, but one day I'm going to kill you and, as you know, I did.'

'What's the point of that story, Pieter?' I asked after he had told it to me in the latrines well after lights-out, while a little joint made a glow between us.

'The point? I suppose he was trying to show me the

163

value of total objectivity. But that led on to his concept of the Overmind, or the Nevermind, as he sometimes called it.'

I laughed. 'What the hell is the "Nevermind"?'

'Well, like as he was loading bodies, he must have been thinking, "Nevermind, I'll get *you* someday, son of a bitch!" but it's more than that.'

'OK, you got me. What?'

'It's that extra mind we've got which when we're, say, screaming with anger, or laughing, or berating somebody, sits up there, evaluating everything. Saying, "This situation calls for Anger. Will Anger achieve what I want? OK, now what level of Anger." Totally objective, see?'

'That's silly.'

'No it isn't. Or, "This situation obviously requires me to be in love. If I pucker my eyes just so and increase heart-beat just so I will appear to be in love." It's like there's another person up there who can always look down and—'

'You mean like a Guardian Angel?'

'Yes, I think some people would call it that.'

'It's all rubbish, of course.'

Actually it's not.

So we went on route marches stoned out of our minds on The Mixture and one day all these rabbits appeared out of nowhere and bounded along with us. We couldn't stop giggling.

Colin Barker was Bungalow Captain. He was the *ouman* who was unofficially in charge of my barracks. He was marching next to us at the time and became suspicious.

And the next time we were sitting in the bog passing a joint under the wall, I looked up and there was Barker peering over the wall. 'So!' he said. 'I thought so. Drugs.'

We were addled with terror as he led us back to the barracks and called a meeting of all the *oumanne* to discuss what to do with us.

Had they decided to rat on us to the Kommandant, we would have been up Shit Creek. The Army has its own prison system for those who break its laws. It's called 'DB', Detention Barracks. Dig this hole. Fill this hole. Run on the spot. That kind of thing.

Luckily, they decided on a worse punishment. Every time we got passes for leave, they made us give the passes to Colin who would ritually tear them up in front of us. We would fake utter despair. Go off for a smoke somewhere.

One weekend when almost everybody was on leave, the Sergeant Major came into the barracks, where we were sitting on a bench chatting about the lamentable lack of dagga. Our supplier, a black kitchen porter called Willie, had gone off to the Transkei to see his wife.

'Tenshun!' I yapped, and we stood to attention.

'Blerry hell,' the Sergeant Major said. 'Where's all the rest?'

'On leave, Sarnmajor.'

'Well, you'll have to do. You're volunteering for escort duty.'

'Are we?' said Pieter

'Don't try be funny, troepie. I want you all packed and ready to move out in two hours.'

'Where are we going, Sarnmajor?'

'Never mind where. You'll be escorting a dangerous black agitator to Robben Island. That's where.'

'Why us? Why aren't the police doing it?' I asked, resentful at the disruption of a peaceful weekend.

'Dunno,' the Sergeant Major said, 'probably *you* blokes are to stave off terrorists. This prisoner is *very* dangerous.'

And he bustled out.

Four

Four people in the back of an army truck. Me and Pieter, sweating in our khaki. Major Bloemsma sweating with frustration in his police blue. Absolom Molapo in his prison uniform just sweating.

To Bloemsma, we were just rifles on legs. He had no idea that we were real people, with real minds.

I had heard of Molapo before, but never met him. The name was familiar, perhaps I had been told Granny's maid's surname at some time. Perhaps I had read of her son's exploits.

Anyway, we sat there in silence while Bloemsma and Molapo exchanged insults like old lovers out on a day-trip.

The truck was driven by a lanky, laconic Afrikaner called Paul De Klerk, who had been the favourite pug of Napoleon's bit, Josephine de Beauharnais, in his previous life and retained many of the best characteristics of that breed, like faithfulness and devotion. He had also, unfortunately, retained the squashed-nose appearance and yappy voice of his canine pre-incarnation.

The journey was an epic one. We couldn't use the train, because Absolom being black, we couldn't sit in the same compartment as our illustrious captive. The same applied to hotels. The trip had to be by truck, and was planned to last five days, with stops at prisons on the way, where we would spend the night.

The first day was a roaring progress through dust and sun. Paul sang incessantly, it was like nasal wallpaper. His repertoire consisted of 'Sarie Marais' and 'Land of Hope and Glory' (in his version: 'Land of Chops and Whoring'). The view out of the back of the truck was like a movie in which the back-projection had run wild. Dusty streets with chickens. Blacks galore, running jerkily from here to there. Cars of singles, couples, families. Endless panorama of veld with scrubby bushes. Koppies full of invisible lions and the ghosts of lions. Brown hilly farms where puzzled sheep looked vainly for dead grass to eat.

We didn't say a single word, that is, me and Pieter. We grunted when we were handed sandwiches. Mostly we listened.

The main difficulty we encountered that day was a bowel- and bladder-relief rota. Luckily Bloemsma had that all worked out. Every couple of hours he would tap on the glass separating us from the Pug and we'd stop. Then he'd point to one of us and say, 'You! Piss break!' and like it or not the person selected would have to walk into the veld and piss. We soon learnt that it was essential to take one's piss-opportunity seriously, as the next one could be four or more hours away.

The first stop, Bloemsma unlocked the cuffs and – click! – bound Pieter to the prisoner. Then he and De Klerk went off into the bushes together. This caused us a few giggles. 'Do you think they're holding each other's?' Pieter asked.

When Absolom's turn came about, Pieter was sent off with him. 'When they get back,' Bloemsma said to me with a superior smile, 'ask your pal if Commies piss red.' I pretended to laugh.

When the very red and embarrassed sunset happened through the dust, we arrived at Welkom.

Who the hell invented this friendly name for this grimy, flea-bitten town? Rambling, rusty two-storey buildings, dead trees. We alighted at the police station. A dead dog reeked in the gutter. Click! Absolom's wrist bound to mine by steel as the Major bounded up the steps to argue about accommodation with a bored desk-sergeant.

He was a hell of a long time. I tried to start a conversation with Molapo. I wanted to express interest, sympathy, show that I was really on his side. 'Um. You're political, aren't you?'

167

'Yes.'

'Oh, um, what did they get you for?'

'Politics!' He's scornful, convinced he's discovered another idiot, albeit an English one. (I had addressed him in English. He always spoke Afrikaans with Bloemsma.)

De Klerk came sniffing round the back of the truck, leaking cigarette-smoke from a number of facial orifices.

'You're not meant to talk to the prisoner,' he said, casually leaning against the tailgate.

'You're not meant to smoke, sarn't,' Pieter replied.

'Ruff, ruff,' he answered, and took a long, slow drag. 'This is a laugh, hey? All us lot just to take this black meat to the slaughterhouse.'

'Slaughterhouse?'

'Ag, sure. They're probably going to hang him.' Pieter and I exchanged worried glances. Absolom looked angry.

'They won't hang me,' said Absolom. 'They need me too much.'

'Don't be so sure. You Commies are all the same. You think you know everything.'

'Why are they going to hang him?' I asked, trying to sound indifferent.

'Treason, I suppose. If we don't hang him, his own lot will.' He laughed in short barks. 'Just think,' he said, 'if I wasn't here I'd be sitting in my lounge with my missus exploring my trousers . . .'

Before he could torture us further with details of his sex-life, Bloemsma returned. 'All right, you lot. Everything's arranged. Let's go.'

The tailgate clashed open and we climbed stiffly out. 'Troepies will share a cell with Molapo. Don't worry, he won't hurt you.' Our apprehension had been misconstrued. 'You and me,' the Major continued, indicating De Klerk, 'are off to the hotel.'

We were escorted to a cell by the desk sergeant, a big

168

sleepy man with a uniform of a crispness unmatched by any Sandhurst graduate's. 'Your room, sirs,' he grinned, doing a bell-boy impersonation. 'Your luggage will be sent up, and if you require anything, just ring the bell.' Then, serious, 'Or if the kaffir tries to escape, *skiet hom dood*.' Which means, shoot him dead.

Our dismay at the bare room with one cot, smell of piss. The bottom half of the wall was painted in a brown gloss to deter graffiti artists who had nevertheless made a scratchy wallpaper of the top half with 'Kiljoy was here', 'Give us a blow, joe', 'Hitler was a rabbit in a previous life', and so on.

'I'll see if I can get you some blankets,' he said.

'Sarn't—' I stopped his exit. 'Did, uh, did the Major give you a key for these?' Pointing to the handcuffs.

He laughed. 'Poor troepie! No. But don't worry. He'll be back in the morning.'

'I need a piss, sarn't.' I did. I was busting.

'Oh, *jislaaik*. You're a bleddy nuisance. Come. You wait,' he motioned Piet to sit.

So Absolom and I went for a pee together. Difficult. Splashing yellow liquid at the same time on the same bit of yellowed porcelain. The sergeant hands on hips leaning against a stall saying, 'I had to get special permission to have Whites and Blacks together in one cell, you know. Now I've got a Black pissing where Whites are supposed to pee. We'll probably all get an infection.'

'These laws aren't easy for any of us,' I said, zipping up. Absolom turned toward me, briefly. We had made a sort of communication at bladder level.

'Don't talk shit, troepie,' said the sarn't. 'Just zip up and come to bed.' He laughed. What a joker.

We returned to the cell. 'I'll have food and blankets sent in to you in a while,' he said, clanging the steel cell-door shut. There was a deep low grind as a piece of steel four inches by three inches by one inch thick cut us off from the world.

Five

A NIGHT IN A CELL WITH ABSOLOM MOLAPO

'They're animals,' I said, finding a place to sit and Absolom sitting of necessity next to me. Piet sat himself on the other side of the black man and there we were, Hear-no-evil, See-no-evil and Speak-no-evil.

'Three monkeys,' said Piet. We laughed.

'Yes, it's funny to you,' Absolom said, 'and when this journey's over you'll go back to your nice little camp and—'

'Look, Mr Molapo, we're not like that lot—'

Now Absolom laughed. '*Mr*? No one has ever called me Mister.'

'Tell me something,' Piet said. 'Do you think *all* Whites are racists?'

'Yes,' he answered. 'A lot of them *say* they're not, but that's just the arrogance of a people so convinced of their superiority, they can afford to be generous.'

'That's not true,' I said. 'What about Paton? Suzman?'

'Don't give me *names*, whitey. Tell me, have any of these liberal heroes married a Black?'

'No but that's because—'

'Breytenbach!' Pieter interrupted.

'You're Afrikaans, aren't you?' Molapo was now talking to Pieter. 'There is no more fervent Christian than a recent convert. Your people regard Breytenbach as a traitor. Are you a traitor, soldier?'

'What?' Piet applied himself to this question with a frown and squeezing of thoughts. 'No,' he answered. 'I think the only option for the Afrikaner is to accept that he has to share his country. I am faithful to my principles.'

'What are your principles, Afrikaner?' Absolom was

beginning to enjoy the situation. The two boys in uniform were the first people he had been allowed to speak to for years – apart from his interrogators and the few words he had been able to exchange with fellow-prisoners.

'I believe there is no meaningful difference between black people and white people; neither physical, nor intellectual. I believe that South Africa will never have peace until we have one man one vote. Those are my principles.'

'I find all this hard to believe. What about you?' He turned to me.

'Well, I believe the same thing. My ancestors, you see, knew all about prejudice. They lived in tiny villages in Russia, carrying on the few trades they were allowed to practise. They were dirt poor. Every now and then Cossacks would arrive and do a little raping and pillaging. That's why I believe only freedom for all the people can bring about peace.'

Absolom looked from one to the other, incredulous. 'I can't believe I'm sitting here in a prison cell with two soldiers talking to me like this. You carry your FNs in one hand and your "principles" in another.'

I lowered my eyes. They travelled gently over the plastic and steel killing-machine made by the Belgians for the Government of South Africa.

'You see we're not all the same. But what could we do? What would we achieve if we had refused to go into the Army?'

'I wonder if you two are a plant. Are they listening to everything we're saying?'

All three went silent, looking around the cell for a microphone.

'I don't think there's anyone listening,' I said, 'and we certainly aren't spies.'

'What are your names?' he asked, and we introduced ourselves.

171

'I'd shake hands,' I said, 'but that would be a little difficult.' We all laughed. Pieter ceremonially shook hands.

'Anyway,' he said, 'you are wrong.'

'What?'

'You are wrong to say that one man one vote would solve all the problems of South Africa.'

'I thought that was what you are fighting for,' I said.

'Yes, that's what I am fighting for. But when that fight is finished, the war will begin.'

'What do you mean?' Piet asked.

'There is one theory that says that South Africa is a myth. The true shape of this country should be a number of independent countries, each with its own constitution and legislature. One for the Zulu, one for the Xhosa, one—'

'But that's Apartheid,' Piet erupted. 'That's what the Nationalists say!'

'Even so there is just a grain of truth in that theory. It falls down when they want to divide the country purely on grounds of colour and give so little of it to the black people.'

'I don't understand,' I said.

'Let me explain it this way: Say one day the Martians arrive in their space ships and conquer Europe with their superior arms. Good. So they rule it for two hundred years and they teach the people how to speak Martian, use Martian skills and so on. And when they see that they have taught the earthmen too much they decide to leave for their own safety. But before they leave they divide the empire into a lot of different countries. A bit of France and Germany mixed together. Half of Spain joined to half of France. And so on.'

'So?'

'So when they leave, they will leave fifty years of civil war behind them, as each language and cultural group reasserts itself and fights for dominance in its own independent country. That's what the colonialists did

172

to Africa. They put the borders wherever it suited them; they put people who hate each other in the same countries. That's why Africa cannot develop in a normal peaceful way until the boundaries are re-defined. Civil war. That's what will happen to South Africa.'

'And you want all this to happen?'

'No. Whatever one *wants*, history dictates what happens and history happens like it happens because of the nature of man. Man's nature does not *seem* to change. But it is evolving.'

'So you are fighting for the right to have a civil war?'

'No. I am just a cog of history. I do what history wants me to do. First we must make freedom. Ask me, rather, what *I* want.'

'All right,' I said. 'What do you want?'

'As a first stage, I want a unitary state in which tribal matters are secondary. I want people to be Azanians first and members of particular tribes or so-called "races" second. Or third. Or forgotten.'

'What, no laws to protect minorities?' Pieter asked.

'What minorities?' Absolom grinned. 'We are *all* Africans: That's the second stage.'

'Go on,' I said.

'The second stage is the unification of Africa. The United States of Africa. That is the message of Robert Sobukwe, my hero, my leader.'

Sobukwe was the imprisoned leader of the PAC. 'Is there a third stage?' I asked.

'Oh yes,' Absolom said. 'The third stage is when the whole world forgets tribalism, nationality. Nationalism is an ugly cancer in the world. It makes wars.'

'Yes,' I said excitedly. Absolom echoed my views.

'But the Boers are always emphasising tribalism. It suits them so to do. Divide and rule. So, transitionally, we may need our civil war . . .' He sighed. 'Anyway, history will decide.'

The door made clanging noises and opened portentously to admit the sarn't, who threw three blankets

173

on to the concrete floor. 'Hallo, troepies!' he said cheerfully. 'Making friends? Watch this kaffir. He's a clever bugger.'

'How are we supposed to sleep?' I asked, pointing to the single bunk.

'You'll find a way,' he smirked. 'Boy,' he shouted out of the door. 'Where's the food?'

A scrawny black man entered with a tray. There were plates of eggs, chops and chips for Piet and me, and a bowl of porridge for Absolom. Paper plates and plastic spoons. Two mugs of coffee and one mug of water. 'Eat up,' said the Sergeant. 'Give us a shout when you're finished.' And they left.

We stared awkwardly at the tray. 'Apartheid food,' Absolom said.

'We'll share it out,' I offered.

'No. You eat the white food. I'll eat this mush.'

'Don't be ridiculous,' Piet said.

'Are you ordering me about, whitey?' Absolom frowned.

A second of startled silence. Then awkward laughter. But Absolom wouldn't accept nor egg, nor chop, nor chip. 'I'm used to this stuff,' he said.

When we had finished, I shouted through the keyhole and a black warder came in and removed the empty plates. As he locked the cell door behind him, Piet asked, 'And is *that* man a traitor, Absolom?'

'No, he's just a fool and he needs the money. Otherwise his family would probably starve. But we'll kill him anyway. That's history.' He sighed, still hungry. 'I want a piss now,' he added.

'Oh hell,' said Piet, 'so do I. I just don't want to shout for that idiot again.'

'Hang on,' said Absolom, and felt under the bed with his free hand. 'Ah yes, here it is.' There was a bucket. It was a quarter-full of ancient piss. Matured in the bucket. Almost pure ammonia. We placed it in the middle of the floor and stood around it and added our three libations, together.

It was like becoming blood brothers, only a lot funnier.

Later we were sitting on the blanket on the floor. Satisfied of stomach, empty of bladder and bowel (the latter had been accomplished off these pages), good companions. We decided to avoid the subject of how we were going to sleep. I asked Absolom, in this spirit of camaraderie, 'Do you think they're really going to hang you?'

I always assume that people I respect aren't bothered by death, because I'm not. As someone with a Nasty Problem – viz. being aware of many of my past lives, remembering many of my deaths – I cannot regard life as anything more than a brief interlude between deaths. Sometimes I guiltily worry that I may even regard life as a rather nifty little holiday, in which I can have all the fun that bodies have. Like spring, and music, and sex, and stuff.

'I don't know,' said Absolom. 'I have had that threat hanging over me' (that was not supposed to be a pun) 'for so long, perhaps it has stopped worrying me.'

'It worries me,' I said, because I wanted him to know that I was a friend and didn't want him to die.

'I was once told a story,' Pieter said.

'Not another one,' I groaned.

'No, listen to this. An old man told me this, Absolom. He was a black witch-doctor who lived near my home in the Eastern Transvaal.

'He was a great liar. He claimed that he was immortal, travelled through space and time in a beaten-up Ford picking up bodies, which he was farming for export to the planet Xichra.'

'I like science fiction,' Absolom grinned. 'Carry on.'

'All right, this is how he told it:

Death and Mary Magee

'I was sixty when I died, Pieter,' he said 'and *au*! it was a surprise to me I can tell you.

'I was harvesting a place in Russia, where the British had managed to achieve many deaths by dashing on their horses at a great bunch of heavily fortified Russians who were well-armed with big cannon. Stupid English!

'So I'm busy with my business, anyway, and I hear a very strange sound above my head. It was something like an eagle being choked by a snake.

'So I looked up and there in a tree, perched on a branch, I saw a woman. She was dressed in torn and ragged clothes and she was weeping like a mad thing.

'Well, I was startled, I can tell you. "What do you want here?" I said. I was very angry. "Go away. I'm working."

' "Who are you?" she asked between her tears. "Are you the One they call the Grim Reaper?"

'Now I was very worried because if she saw the truck – they hadn't invented trucks then, you know, nevermind space ships – my whole cover would be blown. So I said to her, "Come down from there and I'll tell you."

'So she climbed out of the tree, very frightened, and stood there staring at me. "Now," I said, "tell me who you are and why you're here."

' "My name is Mary Magee," she said, her eyes hooded with fear. And she told me her story.

'Well, she used to work as a maid on the estate of Lord Kiloddin in Ireland. Now one of Kiloddin's three sons, the Viscount Sankey, was very delicious and well-proportioned and one day he made love to her.

'Being young and foolish, she fell in love with him and was certain that he loved her.

'Then off he went to fight for the British and of course, as in all these stories, she finds herself pregnant, is found out, refuses to admit who the father is, is thrown out into the snow and searches the whole Crimean War for her lover, ending up on this battlefield where he probably lies.

'"This is a very corny story," I told her, but she just went on weeping. "Take me also, O Reaper," she said. "My life is worth nothing."

'Well of course I was sorry for her but how could I take her with me? I certainly couldn't *kill* her myself, that is not my way.

'"How do you know he is dead?" I asked her. "Have you found his corpse?"

'"No," she said. "Will you not help me to look?"

'I didn't really want to but I agreed to help on condition she helped *me* to load the bodies on to my truck.

'All day we worked, and when the truck was full I took the load to the factory and came back for more. Four loads I took. A good day's work! But it was very tiring, I can tell you. And by dawn, we had not found her lover at all.

'"Well," I said, well satisfied, "my quota is complete and I have to leave the rest. But what must I do with you?"

'She went on her knees and it was pitiful. "Let me look a little longer," she pleaded. "Don't take me away. He's here, I know he is."

'"Bugger it," I said. "I can't leave you here."

'"Get back!" she cried and cringed away from me. I don't know what she thought I was going to do. *I* didn't know what I was going to do.

'Then suddenly she snatched a sword from the hand of a dead Hussar, swung it in a big circle and chopped my head off!'

Absolom and I were laughing hysterically. 'Rubbish, Pieter,' I said. 'If he died in 18-whatever, how could any of the other stories be true?'

'And then *who* told you this?' Absolom asked.

'Wait. It's not finished. This is how Umfaan told it:

'So there I was, looking down at my decapitated body and thinking what a terrific nuisance it was not to have a body when I had all these export orders to fill.

'Here we go again, I thought, and started looking about for the tunnel, and the light, and all the old rubbish. Already I could hear the fear-filled voices of all the dead who lay about me, worried about which way to go next and what to do.

'"Oh dear, here I am dead. What do I do now?" they cry, or "What happens to my children now, I'd better go see," or "That swine who killed me I must find and *haunt*!" And the stupid ones: "Is this Heaven or Hell?" Or whatever. The usual self-pitying blabber. So busy with Regrets and Anger they don't get going for ages.

'Anyway, one of the voices could be heard above all the others. "Go away," it kept shouting. "Leave me alone!"

'"Why don't you shut up," I said, "so we can all get along to wherever we have to get along to?"

'"It's that bloody woman!" he said, referring to that poor murderess Mary Magee, who was staggering about the place with a bloody sword, and who couldn't hear him yelling. She was deaf to the dead like most of the living.

'"Look at her," he said. "She's carrying my child. I can't go on until she stops her bloody moaning and leaves me alone."

'At this stage I had one of my Bright Ideas. "Listen, ex-Viscount," I said, "I'll make a deal with you. How long have you been dead?"

'"Not long, I don't think. I'm not even properly dead yet."

'That's what I thought and there's only one way to free you. Give me your body."

'"Don't be silly. It's full of holes."

'"Never mind the holes. Will you give it to me?"

'"If it gets me away from here, sure. It's yours."

'Well, Umfaan was pretty expert at bodies and life and death and all that and as this one wasn't *too* badly broken, he managed to creep inside and make himself nice and snug and cosy in it. And after a while he learnt how to work its voice box and jaws and lungs and so on. "Groan," he said.

'And Maggie hears this groan and comes running up to the body of her lover. "Eric is that you? You're *alive*, alive!"

'"Groan," said Umfaan again.

'Well, I'll spare you his description of all the moaning and weeping and simply tell you that Mary tended the body until it was well enough to walk, then they took it to the hospital and soon it was as good as new. And after a while they went back to Ireland, had a child, got married, became Lord and Lady Kiloddin, had more babies and lived happily ever after!'

Absolom and I laughed and rolled about the place as best we could in our situation.

'And always after that, Umfaan told me, Mary was convinced that she had killed Death. Until her own happened! Now she's not too sure.'

'What did you say this old witch-doctor was called?' Absolom asked, when he had recovered.

'Umfaan.'

'That's very strange. That was what we called a very old man, a very great witch-doctor who lived with my tribe. My mother told me all about him.'

'Really?' Pieter said, and I could see the little hairs standing up on the back of his neck.

'Yes. And she said that when he got very old and everyone knew he was going to die, he went to his bakkie – which was a beaten-up old Ford Transit – and drove into the sky.'

'Is this true?' I asked.

'That's impossible,' Pieter said, but he wasn't so sure.

*

More night happened, and we talked some more about life and death. I realised something important: While I was not concerned about my own death, the deaths of others bother me for reasons I don't understand. I very much wanted Absolom to live. I felt protective toward him, this thin man who looked ten years older than he was, who had taken the sufferings of his people on himself.

'I think there's a way out of all this,' I said.

Six

By morning we had managed to sleep for two hours, lying cuddled together under three blankets on the chilly floor. We were woken by the black warder coming in with breakfast.

A bowl of porridge for Absolom. Bacon, steak and eggs for the troepies.

Bloemsma bustled into the cell in all his fresh morning crispness, followed by a grinning De Klerk. 'Sleep good?' he asked, all jolliness.

'*Ja*, Major,' we snapped, all military precision, trying to stand and salute.

'*Kom*,' he ordered, and unlocked the cuffs. 'I'll take the kaffir. You two go wash and shave. Christ, what a smell!'

We made our ablutions in the police washroom and the happy little party was ready for the day's journey.

Goodbye Welkom. Welcome to the world.

Vroom, grind of the truck. A chilly morning but it will be hot later. De Klerk steers us on to the Kimberley road. Black children wave as we pass. Then the town vanishes into the past.

More country, more dust in the back-projection. Rolling sheep country this, parched and bare to the bones. A skeleton of a country. How can people fight and lie and die for *this*?

Bloemsma whistles along to the barely heard singing of the driver. *'My Sarie Marais is so ver van my hart, Ek hoop om haar weer to sien, Daar onder in die mielies by die groen Doringboom, Daar woon my Sarie Marais . . .'* It's a Boer War song. The soldier is leaving his little love and is off to fight the British. The hated British who have invaded his country and put his family into concentration camps. This land has seen plenty of blood.

I cradle my rifle on my knees, my death machine. Pieter's profile against the back-projection of vanishing road. I realise that I love him.

Absolom and Bloemsma against the shiny, shifting shadows from the front of the truck, shadowed by the future. I love them both, too.

The Angel of Death is hovering over us.

'It's going to be a nice day,' Bloemsma announces for Absolom's benefit. 'Look at that land out there. This is God's country, Molapo. Not yours or mine.'

'That's true,' Absolom says sadly. 'We will all die one day. We cannot say this is mine or this is yours. Everything is only borrowed.'

'Good heavens, I don't believe my ears. You aren't religious, are you? Communists don't believe in God.'

'Maybe they don't but I do. Not the same God as yours, I'm sure. My God loves Blacks as well as Whites.'

'There is only one God, Molapo. And he had a son. And that son had disciples. Tell me, Molapo, were any of those sons black?'

'We don't know,' Absolom answered. 'The only thing we know for sure is that none of them were Christians.'

'What the hell are you talking about?'

'They were Jews, Major, all of them. Till the day he died Christ was a Jew.'

'That's blasphemy, you bloody Commie. You twist everything for your own benefit.'

Absolom doesn't reply and I give him a secret smile.

He knows how far he can go. Making Bloemsma angry was a good game once. It's no longer appropriate.

Vrrgrr up a hill grrowl crunch of low gear down the hill again. *'Daar onder in die Mielies by die groen Doringboom.'*

'Piss break!' Bloemsma commands, raps on the window. Raps on our pounding hearts. We trio have sweat breaking out. Grind stop. 'You!' he commands and with great relief I leap out and piss in the bushes.

Off again in glum silence. Bloemsma is bored. He has tried whistling, but this was as irritating to him as it was to us. He has made intricate tapping noises with his fingers and exhausted all the permutations. So he discovers that Pieter and I exist. 'You, troepies – where do you come from?'

'I'm from Johannesburg, Major,' I snap in military response.

'I'm from Ventersdaal in the Eastern Transvaal, Major,' Pieter snaps.

'Lovely country,' the Major says, memories in his eyes. 'We used to go there for holidays when I was a kid. The Kruger Park, Blyde River Canyon, God's Window, all that. *Magtig!* It's all proof of God.'

'Ja, Major.'

'Do you know Pilgrim's Rest?' he asks Pieter. I have ceased to exist for him. Johannesburg is labelled Concrete Jungle in his mind, and that's that.

'Ja, Major.'

'You see Molapo, this is what your lot will never understand. Our people went to Pilgrim's Rest nearly a hundred years ago, when it was a swampy little place full of malaria, fevers, everything. They found gold there and civilised the whole area for miles around. They drained the swamps so it was fit for people to live there. They built churches and schools and gave all the poor Blacks who already lived there work to do. And when the gold ran out they went off to the Witwatersrand – your place,' he nodded at me – 'found more gold and civilised all round there. You Blacks don't understand what we have suffered for this country. You don't understand *gratitude*.'

Absolom laughs softly.

The Major is drowning in memories. '*Ja*, our holidays round there. My pappie told me all the history when he showed us that place. And to see that little town there just as it was in the early years of this century – it's preserved, you see – it's wonderful. All those lovely little houses with corrugated-iron roofs.

'We travelled all round there, every year. Mammie and Pappie would pack us all in the Chevy and we'd leave the farm with my cousin and the whole family – me, my three sisters, Tannie as well as my parents – would drive off to the sunset. *Ja*.' He sighs.

Pedigree growl. A Mercedes full of screaming children and harassed parents appears in the back-projection. Massive suitcases are strapped to the luggage rack. It sits on our tail for a little, then pulls away and overtakes. 'You see that, Molapo?' He points to them as they vanish into the past. 'That was how we went on holidays. Only not in a Mercedes. We weren't so bleddy rich.'

He muses for a while. We maintain a sympathetic silence and wish the monologue would end. I don't want to know about Bloemsma. I don't want to know if he has a wife, or children.

'Did you ever play games when you went on holiday?' he asks us in general. Absolom snorts. Piet and I nod. 'Did you ever play "Cars"?' I grin, recognising the game. It had caused bloodshed between Plowsky and me, more than once. Piet looks puzzled. 'It's easy. Look, I'll be Fords. You, troepie, can have Volkswagens – pointing to me – 'You other troepie can have Fiats.' He turns to Absolom. 'This is a *game*, Molapo. We white people like to play games.'

'I know that.'

'You play as well. You can have Mercedes. All right?

183

Every one you see of your car, you get one point for. If anyone else shouts the name of your car first you lose a point. Everyone clear?'

The soldiers nod. The prisoner growls.

Four grown men sitting tense in the back of an army truck, almost hanging over the tailgate, waiting to play a children's game. Wanting to win.

'Aargh! Ford! Ford! I got one!' the Major shouts.

First point to the Security Force.

'Where? Where?'

'Just passed us. Didn't you see?'

'Volksie! There goes a Volksie!'

'Where? Aha, Mercedes. Wake up, Molapo! You've lost a point already.'

'There's a Fiat. One to me.'

'That's not a Fiat. That's one of those Japanese things.'

'Fiat!'

'Never mind, I got a Ford. There! Do you see?'

'You've counted that one already.'

'No I haven't. You see, Molapo? It's exciting, isn't it?'

'There's a Mercedes.'

'What?'

'Yes, there. See? Another one. And another one.' Absolom is grinning like a child with a new pellet gun. Pointing to a car transporter, laden with new Mercedes.

'Bullshit! That's cheating.'

Pieter and I double up with laughter.

'You can't count that.' The Major shouts. He's purple.

'Look,' says Pieter. 'Ford alert! Ford alert!'

'One less to you, Major,' Absolom says gravely.

'Volksie! Volksie!'

RAPRAP. 'That's enough, kiddies. Piss break!'

'Don't like to lose, Major, do you?' Absolom asks sweetly.

'You watch it, prisoner. You!' – he means me – 'take this.' He unclasps and reclasps. Absolom and I are Siamese-twinned again. 'De Klerk and me are going for

184

a piss.' His little revenge. So you lot are going to have to bloody wait.

So now. This means. Electric shock through three hearts. Oh shit. He leaps lightly over the tailgate. *'Kom, De Klerk! Ons gaan piss.'* Off they go. Like Jack and Jill.

Reluctantly three pairs of eyes swivel until they meet. Do I want to do this? 'Let's get going,' Absolom says. But when we try to move the handcuffs impede.

'What are we going to do about these?'

'We have to get them off. Quickly,' Absolom replies.

'He's got the bloody key with him.'

'Shit. Can you shoot them off?'

'If we do they'll rip your hand to shreds,' I answer dully.

Look round for Pieter. He's sighting through his rifle. Peering at the slope of the hill through two crossed hairlike pieces of metal. At Jack and Jill. Who have finished peeing. They zip up, joking about this and that. They turn around. Simultaneously, they see the rifle pointing in their direction. The Major stares uncomprehendingly for a little. Then he waves as if to push the barrel aside. I crouch next to Pieter and sight too. Fear leaps into two faces. Absolom says quietly, 'You don't have to do this, you know.'

Bangbang

Jack and Jill fell down the hill.

Pieter drops his rifle, runs up to the twitching bodies. Frisks the Major. Returns with the key. Releases us with shaking sweaty hands. We jump out and leap into the cab. I slip into the driving seat. We're all shaking. Our khaki has dark sweat patches. Absolom sits in the middle. Piet closes his door. Then he opens it again and is sick.

One

Grr vroom. Army truck in midday Free State with its party of fugitives. It smells of petrol and sweat. We are bugs in a bottle looking through the glass and fancying we can fly to freedom.

We are harbingers of death. Blood on our hands.

'Where are we going?'

'We have to dump this truck,' Absolom says. 'They will miss us by tonight, by the next stop. They will find the bodies. They will search the country like wolves. We have to steal a car somewhere.'

'Where?'

Pieter sits on the other side of Absolom. He looks like an accident victim in a coma. Absolom and I find the future our responsibility. 'What's the next place on this road?'

'Pieter, see if there's a map.'

'What?' He starts back to life.

'Pieter, look for a map.'

He searches the glove compartment which is full of papers and a black, smelly pipe. Everything is covered in shreds of tobacco. A map. 'Bultfontein,' he says.

'What about clothes?' I ask. 'We can't escape in these uniforms.'

'We'll find something,' Absolom reassures.

'And then what?'

'We'll get ourselves to Botswana. I've got friends there.'

And so I drive. We decide to get near to Bultfontein and hide the truck somewhere. Then at nightfall, to find a car, clothes.

I drive. What will. How will we. I didn't know I could. Pieter. Am I right. There is no. Will we make it.

Absolom in the middle. Will it. Is this my. Oh my people. Will they believe. Thank God. What am I. These two angels, so young, so stupid. History. Killed you, Mother. I'm going to. You'll see.

Pieter at the end. Am I. Umfaan! You bastards. Historical inevitability. I pulled the trigger. I pulled the trigger. I pulled the trigger. Historical inevitability. Oh Tom. What am I now.

I drive. The sky is going pink. Dog-eared clouds picking up the pinkness puffing trails about them as they breathe in and out. Blood-spattered. Volksie. Mercedes. Fiat. Three points.

The silence in the cab like soup, I am drowning.

Clatter. What? Clatter.

'Look! There!' Pieter is very awake.

'What? Where?'

'Helicopter! There!'

'I see it,' Absolom said.

There is where the present tense changes to the past tense. It is all past from now on.

Because the helicopter was shadowing us. The future was ended. Suddenly there were no cars on the road. The game was over.

'Do you think they're shadowing us?' Pieter wanted confirmation.

'Yes,' said Absolom. 'They must have found the bodies.'

'We should have hidden them,' I said.

'What should we do now?' Pieter asked. We were still pathetically sure that Absolom could work a miracle, but he couldn't. 'Keep driving,' he said and after a while we rounded a corner and it was sunset by then and half dark and hard to see but we could make out the roadblock and the huddled shapes of frightened police and army pointing their guns at us and bang-bang and I tried to turn the truck around. 'Give me the gun,' Absolom said, but the truck lurched and two wheels went into the air and then we were over and.

And then there was a prison hospital and somebody shaking me and asking me questions.

Two

While I lay there in that hospital bed, while my bones knitted together and flesh grew again where it had been pared off and I wrote this, Pieter lay in the room next to me. He had been dented, an arm was holed and his left ear was in shreds.

Brigadier Maartens entered, shooed the guard away. Maartens was head of BOSS, the Bureau of State Security.

Pieter opened an eye and stared at Fate.

'We are very proud of you, my boy,' said the Brigadier. He was a very large man in every sense. Massive eyebrows, like moths, hovered below a swatch of steel-grey hair.

Pieter had been dreaming of virgins begging for his attention. He snatched at the bedclothes and pulled them over the stick-insect (his name for his willie. He was being unfair to himself, as it was quite a normal size) and hoped that it didn't show. 'Proud? Why?'

'You and the other fellow – the Jewboy – fighting all those terrorists. Capturing Molapo. He was a very dangerous man, you know.'

'Was—?'

'We hanged him two days ago. Before he died he confessed everything.'

'I don't understand.'

'Of course you understand, my boy. He explained how you made a stop and were attacked by terrorists, his friends. Then he captured you and you very cunningly drove him right into our trap!'

'That's not—'

'Silence!,' said the Brigadier. 'Did I give you permission to speak?'

'No, Brigadier, but—'

'You had better be silent, my boy. The Jewboy has been saying some strange things to us. He was obviously delirious. We do not intend to believe his rambling.'

'But—'

'Silence! Listen to me carefully, Mostert. As far as we are concerned you two are heroes. Any other story is not to be contemplated. Your actions have given us the excuse to hang a very dangerous man. There were two murders committed, you know.'

'But—'

'But absolutely fucking nothing,' he said, and his eyebrows came to within inches of Pieter's face. 'There is no possibility that two members of the South African Defence Forces would assist a Communist to escape. One of them an Afrikaner too! Do you understand?'

He nodded and the Brigadier drew away. 'Now you don't want to dangle at the end of a rope, do you?'

'No, Brigadier.'

'Then listen carefully.' He grabbed a chair and it vanished under his bulk. 'We have tapes, you see. Tapes of your stupid friend's delirious rubbish. We don't want those tapes to get into the wrong hands, you see. Like the press, or the police.

'This means from now on you are *mine*. See? From now until the end of your life you are working for BOSS. You will do what I say when I say. If not, you and your Jewboy friend will dangle. You will wait for my instructions. Is that clear?'

Pieter nodded. He was very pale.

'Needless to say, you won't tell the Jewboy this. He is far more useful as your friend. He will lead you to the enemies of the state. You will just tell him that the idiots have made a mistake, that Molapo protected you two. Now, aren't you lucky?'

Pieter nodded, whispered, '*Ja*, Brigadier.'

'That's what I want to hear.' And he left.

As soon as Pieter could walk he hobbled next door to see me.

'Hey,' I said, scattering grapes. 'Are you all right?'

'Nearly,' he said, and sat gingerly on the metal fold-up chair by my bed. 'They've hanged Absolom—'

'Shit!' I said. I had this heavy feeling of Fate – History, as Absolom would have called it – coming into the room and sitting on my chest.

'Murder, terrorism, whatever,' Pieter answered my unasked question.

'Bastards. I suppose we're next.'

'No we're not,' he said, avoiding my eyes.

'Why not?'

'Just keep your mouth shut, all right. Keep your mouth shut and we'll be heroes. Absolom made sure of that.'

'*Heroes*?'

'We have to survive, don't we? We have to keep going. For the Revolution. We're no good to anyone dead. Just don't ask me any more questions. Don't ask me any more questions!'

191

I stared at him, trying to penetrate the skin and hair and bone between his mind and mine. But he looked down at the floor. 'All right,' I said finally, and left it there.

When we are both better we are going back to Ventersdaal. We are going to look for an ancient black man who drives a beaten-up old Ford Transit. And after we have asked him Why a few times we are going to beg him to let us help him. I rather fancy being free in time and space, to wander, harvesting, harvesting.